T0167087

THE
LEGEND
OF
HUMANITY:

The Remaining One

Alexander Rebelle

authorHOUSE®

AuthorHouse™
1663 Liberty Drive
Bloomington, IN 47403
www.authorhouse.com
Phone: 1-800-839-8640

First published by AuthorHouse   01/20/2012

ISBN: 978-1-4685-4504-3 (sc)
ISBN: 978-1-4685-4503-6 (ebk)

Library of Congress Control Number: 2012901092

Printed in the United States of America

Contents

Part II

Author's Note

In my mind, there is an entire universe. As I stated in the author's notes from my first novel, *The Harmony Passion*, the stories to be told out of my universe are as numerous as the number of stars in the sky as observed from the planet Earth. My eagerness to tell these stories has driven me to find a passion in artistic expression: it has changed the way I think and look at the universe we all live in. I long to create, whether it be through music, through art, through poetry, or through literature. The desire I feel to tell stories and to create is ever-present.

But after the success of *The Harmony Passion*, I learned that, unfortunately, much of what I put into my work is often lost on the casual reader. While my work does have its share of entertainment value, what I do in my work is to put forth my best effort toward creating literature in a classic mold. Classic literature has captivated my interest since I first realized my passion for writing. The perception of *The Harmony Passion* as a gripping drama has taught me much about the formula for a successful work since I wrote it. I had put together what I believed to be a work of social commentary, symbolism, and themes that were universal, but, as I soon came to realize, a vast majority of it was lost on the average reader. So, with this stated, in this author's note, I hope to bring readers to realize that in literature, there is far more to the story than simply what happens next. Everything in literature has a meaning to it. Nothing is ever arbitrary or written simply for entertainment value. And, as an author, I believe strongly in the concept of, 'show and don't tell.' The narrative style in my work relies on the main character of each particular segment of each chapter for information. There is no single point of view in my work. The narration comes from within the mind of each character. In *The Harmony Passion*, the first segment of the first chapter is shown to you through the mind of Apollo. How would Apollo know what Jeff and Steve are thinking, and what reason would Apollo have to abruptly think about his life story? He can't read minds and he certainly doesn't know he's part of a fictional story being observed by people from a different universe that can read minds. That's the formula for my work. I know it forces the reader to have to figure everything out for himself or herself, but, in my opinion, that's the way literature should be. I always laugh at people when they criticize *The Harmony Passion* for not having a single omniscient narrator. So, in conclusion, this is what I try to do in my work. I cannot say for sure if I've done any of this in either *The Harmony Passion* or in this work, but I would like to let it be known that it was certainly my intention.

In this work, I've chosen to reveal to you a story from the universe in my mind that has taught me much about my own self. If you're familiar with *The Harmony Passion*, then nearly half a century has passed on the planet Earth from the time *The Harmony Passion* ended to the time this new story begins. That's all the omniscient free information you're going to get. I hope you enjoy the story. Thank you very much.

Part I:

1:

I: The craft trembled violently and the cabin went dark. The young pilot looked down at the dashboard, seeing the lifeless instruments and meters before him. He cursed out loud and grabbed a hold of the throttle, attempting one last time to revive the craft. But there was no effect. The young pilot looked out the view port before him as the craft entered the planet's atmosphere.

Flames engulfed the vessel. The young pilot ripped his helmet off, removing a glass cover from a small red button before him. He placed his finger over it and waited, breathing in and out again and again. Several moments passed.

He pressed the button. His chair rocketed out of the craft and the parachute immediately deployed. He slowly began to drift down to the ground.

As he fell closer and closer to the ground, he checked his sidearm to make sure it was armed.

Several moments passed before he hit the ground. Once he did, he quickly cut himself loose and made a run across the field he had landed in. He came to a road and immediately dove for cover behind a bush as a wheeled transport approached him. It had flashing lights and an armed turret.

The transport passed by and the pilot ran across the road, coming to a small river that ran beneath a bridge and into the woods. The pilot followed the river upstream deep into the woods, eventually coming to a small waterfall. He sat down on a rock there to rest as his mind raced.

He looked at the waterfall. There was a cave behind it. The young pilot rose from the rock and waded through the pool at the base of the waterfall, closing his eyes as he walked beneath the cascade of water to enter the cave. He paused for a moment to think, but then he heard footsteps coming from deeper in the cave. He drew his sidearm, aiming it into the darkness ahead of him.

"Who's there?" he demanded. "Don't take another step or I'll shoot."

A light shone on him. It was blinding. He couldn't see. He felt himself being grabbed and pulled deeper into the cave. His weapon was knocked out of his hand. The light went out and he could see nothing. He fell forward and felt the ground beneath him begin to move. He climbed to his hands and knees and stared at the sight before him in the dim lighting of a crudely carved hallway.

Her clothing was soiled and torn, and her face and hair were dirty. She held a small pistol in her hands, pointing it down at him as he looked up at her from his hands and knees.

"Maski beshi vey?" she demanded. "Maski?"

The pilot raised his hands in the air. "Interstellar Union," he said. "Earth. United Nations."

The woman repeated the demand. "Maski beshi vey?" she asked.

"Don't shoot," said the pilot. "I'm from Earth. United Nations."

"What part of Earth?" asked the woman. She spoke English.

"United States of America," said the pilot. "United States Planetary Defense Force."

"What are you doing so deep into enemy territory?" asked the woman. "This system was never a part of the Interstellar Union."

A second woman clad in a dark green uniform walked up behind the woman with the pistol.

"Vaski kamayela?" asked the uniformed woman. "Maski bela sune?"

"Amerikán," said the armed woman. "Shu hayela."

The uniformed woman pointed down the hallway. "Vandán," she said. "Tura."

"Up," said the armed woman. "Get up."

The pilot rose to his feet, keeping his hands in the air. The woman kept the pistol aimed at him. "Walk," she said. "Straight ahead. Walk."

The pilot began walking down the hallway. He came to a door on the right side.

"Stop," said the armed woman. She walked up to the control panel next to the door and punched in a code. The door slid open. It was a room with a single table and a chair. "Sit down," said the woman. The pilot sat in the chair. The woman holstered her weapon. "Name?" she asked.

"Lance Corporal Jason Constantine," said the pilot. "United States Planetary Defense Force."

"If you're from the Interstellar Union, then why are you here?" asked the woman. "What reason could your commanders possibly have to send you this deep into the Vazonian Empire?"

"I'd die before I'd tell you," said Jason. "My people believe in freedom, and we fight to restore freedom to the galaxy. As far as I'm concerned, you can go to hell."

"Spare us the trouble of having to resort to more drastic forms of interrogation," said the woman. "We have no interest in seeing the Interstellar Union fall to the Vazonian Empire. We are not your enemy. It would concern us, however, if you're something other than a Union pilot. The Vazonian Empire would want nothing more than to compromise our own goals by deceiving us. So tell me: why were you sent to this planet?"

Jason said nothing. He looked up at her defiantly.

"We are not your enemy," said the woman. "We despise the Vazonian Empire. I'm asking you to convice us that you're not one of them. Why were you sent to this planet?"

"Piracy," said Jason. "Piracy is disrupting the supply chain in the Interstellar Union. Everyone knows that. This is where the raids come from."

The woman nodded. "So they do," she said. She paused. "This very well could be considered an act of espionage against the Vazonian Empire. The penalty for that is death. Are you aware of that?"

"I follow my orders and I'm not afraid," said Jason. "And my orders are not to talk to the Vazonian Empire."

"I repeat myself," said the woman. "I am not Vazonian. I despise the Vazonian regime. All of us do. If I were Vazonian, you'd wish you were dead."

II: All was silent in the assembly room as the footsteps echoed louder and louder, drawing all eyes toward the chamber doors in anticipation of the arrival. The doors flew open. A woman stepped into the room, jumping up onto the assembly table and beginning to pace back and forth across it, looking down as she held her chin in the palm of her right hand. Her body was draped in a robe that was ice blue in color and was held closed over her body by a golden sash at her waist. She stood up straight and threw her fist into the palm of her other hand.

[I want to know who,] she said. She spoke her language sternly. [I want to know who is responsible for the destruction of the outpost.]

The room was silent. The woman turned sharply at the far end of the table to look down the length of it. [You will tell me now,] she yelled. [You will tell me how they learned of the outpost, and you will tell me who is responsible for its destruction.]

A uniformed man spoke up. [General Drefán is in charge of the operation, your highness,] he said. [I would speculate that his strategy and thinking were not as sound as he thought them to be.]

The Queen stepped up to the uniformed man and looked down at him. [Bring him to me,] said the Queen. [Bring him to me now. I will personally remind him of what it means to serve the Vazonian Empire.]

[At once your highness,] said the man. He rose from his seat and hurried out the door.

The Queen stepped forward and looked down at a woman with an electronic right eye.

[Director Zerpanya,] said the Queen. [Have you located the fighter craft that crashed on the planet?]

[Yes, your highness,] said Zerpanya. [It's American in design. We found that the pilot did eject and then landed in a field near the Troyán Mountains.]

[Have you located the pilot?] asked the Queen.

[No, your highness,] said Zerpanya. [But the area is being searched as we speak. I have ordered Ven Thar not to rest until the pilot is found. I would caution you, though, that the resistance is in the area. We do not know the exact location of the outpost, but if the resistance finds the pilot, they will most definitely attempt to keep him from us.]

[The resistance,] said the Queen. [The filth of the empire. May Xiaf condemn them to eternity in darkness. Director, have you located their central base of operations?]

[We have not, your highness,] said Zerpanya. [Very few in the resistance know of its location. We do not even know which planet the base is on.]

[If this is the case, then I'm personally assigning you to find it,] said the Queen. [That is your new focus: Ven Thar will now be committed to finding the resistance. Locate the Shadow Base and we will destroy them. We will end this.]

[Yes, your highness,] said Zerpanya. [I will begin the search immediately.]

[Everyone else, you disgust me,] said the Queen. [Get out of here.]

The rest of the assembly hurried out of the room. Zerpanya remained seated. The Queen looked down at her from atop the table.

[I want to silence their resistance now,] said the Queen. [See to it that you find their base.]

[By Xiaf, I promise you that I will find them,] said Zerpanya.

[You're dismissed,] said the Queen.

Zerpanya rose from her seat and walked out of the assembly room.

III:

A uniformed man with four silver stars on his shoulders sat behind the desk in the office with a document in front of him. He reviewed the document as another uniformed man with three silver stars on his shoulders spoke.

"One casualty, sir," he said. "Lance Corporal Jason Constantine. It's uncertain as to whether or not he ejected and landed safely."

"From what we've seen so far," said the Four-Star General, "the Vazonian Empire has never kept quiet when they've managed to kill or capture one of our men in their own territory."

"I would agree, sir," said the Three-Star General. "Their silence is odd: they seem to have a certain arrogance and pride about them. I'd never expect them to let this go unnoticed."

"What do you think this could mean, General?" asked the Four-Star General. "As it is, we understand very little about this enemy, but my gut tells me there's something more to this."

"What if," said the Three-Star General, "He ejected safely and they simply haven't found him? What if this soldier is hiding away somewhere hoping we'll come to take him home? The men in his unit are begging us to go looking for him. They all seem convinced that he's good enough to avoid capture. They say he's a very smart young man: son of a psychologist."

"It doesn't matter," said the Four-Star General. "No one is that good in this day and age. With the surveillance technology the Vazonian Empire has, no one could possibly stay elusive long enough for a mission to recover him."

"In my experience, anything is possible in warfare," said the Three-Star General.

"How could a soldier elude capture so deep into enemy territory on his own?" asked the Four-Star General. "If he weren't alone, it would be a different story."

"But how do we know for sure?" asked the Three-Star General. "Our intelligence just isn't good enough."

"I'm well aware," said the Four-Star General. "The Union's intelligence-gathering methods are grossly ineffective and have been for nearly a decade. If I could command Union military operations, there are many things I would change. But the Union would never allow a general from Earth into such a high position of command."

"True," said the Three-Star General. "The politics of the Union have frustrated us since we joined it."

There was a pause. "But perhaps, General, that could work out in my favor," said the Four-Star General. "What if we don't have to go through the Interstellar Union at all?"

"What do you mean, sir?" asked the Three-Star General.

"I have an idea," said the Four-Star General. "The Union is only an alliance. It's nothing more than that."

IV: Jason sat alone in the room as he waited for the woman to return. The door opened and both she and the uniformed woman entered.

"Allow me to introduce myself," said the uniformed woman. "My name is General Hatshenya. I am the leader here. Right now, it is obvious to me that we all share a common goal: to see a galaxy at peace and free of the Vazonian regime. Would you agree that your people share this goal?"

"I would agree," said Jason. "We fight for freedom."

"We, too, fight for freedom," said General Hatshenya. "That is our goal, that is our mission, and we have vowed never to rest until we have brought an end to the Vazonian Empire. And as is such, I have decided to offer you an opportunity: you will fight with us, and, should the chance ever arise, we will return you to your people safely."

"You want me to fight with you?" asked Jason. "And why would I ever agree to fight with anyone other than my own people?"

"It's simply a risk you'll have to take," said General Hatshenya. "Let me enlighten you as to what we are: we are No Kasanosi, an underground network of individuals that have all become frustrated with pledging our allegiance to the Queen and her God. She's a tyrant that has cast aside all her people once stood for in order to gain control of the galaxy. We all seek to overthrow her, and we all seek to restore freedom and sovereignty to the galaxy: in both the Vazakanian Empire and in all the worlds she now controls beyond that."

"What's the Vazakanian Empire?" asked Jason.

"That is the true identity of her people," said Hatshenya. "They are not Vazonians. They are Vazakanians, the children of nature's beauty. There are some Vazakanians right here in this very outpost. You will most likely meet them if you agree to work with us."

"So you're a resistance group," said Jason. "Aren't you?"

"We're a revolution," said Hatshenya. "Now will you fight for us, or will you force us to keep you in detainment? The choice is yours. Consider your options carefully. What will you do?"

"I guess I have no choice," said Jason. "I'll fight for you as long as you keep your word that you'll get me home."

"We will keep our word," said the General. "Now come with us. We'll bring you to your quarters."

Jason rose from the chair and began following General Hatshenya down the hallway. They came to another door and Hatshenya opened it, revealing a large and dimly lit command center. Several of the people inside glanced at Jason suspiciously as he passed them by. He tried not to make eye contact with any of them.

The General led Jason to another door, opening it and leading him into a corridor lined with doors on both sides. They came to a door toward the middle of the corridor and Hatshenya knocked on it. After a moment, the door opened.

She had long blonde hair, emerald green eyes, and she was dressed in a thinly woven robe that was white in color but dirty and stained, and it was held closed over body by a grey sash at her waist.

"This is your roommate," said General Hatshenya. "Her name is Danya. She is best suited to quickly training new members of the resistance. She will do her best to make you feel comfortable. I'll leave you now, and you two can get better acquainted with each other."

Hatshenya walked away. Jason stepped inside the room and Danya closed the door. She sat down on the bed in the left side of the room. All was silent for a moment, but then Jason spoke.

"Pleasure to meet you," said Jason. "My name is Jason. What exactly do I call you?"

"I'm Danya," said the young woman. "When you're not in training. In training, I'm your Commander."

"I understand," said Jason. He paused. "Where are you from, Commander?"

"You're not in training now," said Danya. "I'm Danya to you now."

"I apologize," said Jason. "Where are you from, Danya?"

"It used to be called the Vazakanian Empire," said Danya. "But it's not called that anymore."

"Well, I'm sorry to hear that," said Jason. He paused. "I'm unfamiliar with this side of the galaxy though. I'm not quite sure where the Vazakanian Empire is."

"It's the original empire," said Danya. "Before the Queen set out to conquer the galaxy, she lived in the Vazakanian Empire. That's where I'm from."

"So what's the story behind all of this?" asked Jason. "How did the Queen become the Queen?"

"It's a long story," said Danya. She nodded. "Long and complicated."

"I have patience," said Jason. "My people know very little about the Vazonian Empire."

"It all happened because of corrupt politics and religion," said Danya. "It was a dark time in the Vazakanian Empire. People were starving, and there was crime, there was disease, and there was desperation. The people were vulnerable to anything that would give them false hope.

Jonarka was the founder and leader of a business called Vazonya. Vazonya manufactured many things for the military. The company made weapons, armor, warships, and many other things that the military could use. But what Jonarka did was to begin speaking out politically during the depression. The sponsorship of politicians had begun long ago, but now that the people were desperate, the need for a source of funding for political campaigns was greater than ever. Jonarka bought more and more politicians through sponsorship with every election until Vazonya controlled the government. And that was when she grabbed power. She offered the desperate people an ancient religion with a god called Xiaf, and she said faith in Xiaf could unite the empire and give it strength. And the people decided to listen and fulfill that prophecy for her."

2:

I: Zerpanya watched the monitor as she eased the spacecraft down into the mountain hangar. She cut the power to the thrusters and then began preparing the vessel for her exit. The cabin pressure began to equalize, and once it fully had, she rose from her seat and lowered the ramp. She exited the craft, finding a large formation of soldiers standing at attention with an officer at the front of the formation.

[Director Zerpanya,] he said. [This is unexpected. What brings you here to Troyanya?]

Zerpanya walked up to the General and looked him in the eyes. All was silent as she did so. It was quiet enough to hear the faint sound of the focusing motors in her artificial right eye.

[Don't play stupid with me, Kufán,] said Zerpanya. [You're here for one reason and one reason alone. Do you remember what that reason is?]

[Of course I do,] he said. [We're here to locate the Shadow Outpost in the region.]

[The Queen has had enough,] said Zerpanya. [She wants to destroy them once and for all. I've been sent here to get the job done. Under my leadership, we will find the Shadow Outpost, and it will lead us to the Shadow Base. And we will do it immediately. Do you understand me?]

[Yes ma'am,] said the General. [What are your orders?]

[You will give me access to all information and data you've gathered regarding the location of the base,] said Zerpanya. [I will review it and I will decide what happens next. Thank Xiaf that the Queen does not punish you for your incompetence.]

[At once, Director,] said the General. [Our intelligence center is right this way.]

Zerpanya began following the General. She waited until they got into the hallway away from the soldiers. [How does it feel, Kufán?] she asked. [Do you enjoy what came of your attempt to oust me from my position?]

The General didn't answer.

[I asked you question, my love,] said Zerpanya. [Did you not hear me?]

[I enjoy my new position, Director,] said the General. [I feel it is for the greater good of the Vazonian Empire.]

[Did I detect sarcasm in your voice?] asked Zerpanya. [Sarcasm won't do when a field general addresses the Director of Ven Thar. You've just been demoted again. General Blayán is now your superior.]

[This is our intelligence center,] said the General. [You have access to all the information we have.]

Zerpanya looked at the room full of computer consoles and monitors.

[Leave me,] she said. [I will go to work immediately. No hard feelings, my love.]

II:

Jason opened his eyes to the sound of a closing door. He watched as Danya turned from the door and looked at him. He stared at her. She was no longer dressed in the dirty white robe. Instead, she now she wore an outfit of two pieces: the top half of which had long sleeves of sheer fabric that opened up wide like bells at her wrists and was open in front like a jacket, but cropped short far from her waist to leave the better portion of her midsection bare. The garment had a wide neckline as well that opened up toward her shoulders, covering only enough of her breasts as to conceal their very tips from view. A grey sash threaded through a number of loops around the bottom of the garment to hold it closed there, tying tightly in front beneath her breasts, seeming almost to lift them up before his eyes.

The bottom half of the outfit was a skirt-like garment that was somewhat pleated, the pleating being only subtly pronounced, and it was very short in length. There was also quite a bit of distance between it and the top half of the outfit. It was revealing to say the least.

Jason could not help but stare at the sight. He noticed that she also wore a holster on the grey sash with a small pistol on her left side. On her feet, there was a pair of black boots that extended up to her knees.

"I certainly hope you're rested," she said. "As a fighter, you have to wake up on time."

"My apologies," said Jason. "I'll do my best not to oversleep in the future."

"You don't do your best here," said Danya. She shook her head. "You do what you're told here. And right now, I'm telling you that you have to wake up on time. But because it's your first day, you will not be disciplined. So come with me: you need energy for the day."

"What do your people eat?" asked Jason. "I've never eaten any alien food."

Danya paused to look at him. "We eat what we can," she said. "Whatever we can to stay well-nourished."

Danya opened the door to the room and began walking down the hallway. Jason followed behind her, continuing to ponder the way she was dressed. She led him to a dimly lit open room full of low tables and stools. There were a number of people in the room. Most were sitting together in groups laughing and talking, and some were eating, and there were others playing some sort of card game.

Danya led him over to a vacant table. He sat down and she went over to a table in the corner of the room, removing two of some sort of red-colored fruit and placing them each on slabs of wood. She brought both slabs over to the table and sat down across from him.

"This is Maluna," said Danya. "Grows on a special kind of tree."

"Is it like a fruit?" asked Jason.

"I don't know what a fruit is, so I couldn't tell you," said Danya. "It's Maluna."

Jason paused. "May I ask some questions about this resistance?" he asked.

"As long as you do it fast," said Danya. "We have a lot to do today."

"Then why have I never heard of this resistance?" asked Jason. "How long ago did it form?"

Danya shrugged her shoulders "The Queen makes sure we're never seen or heard of," she said. She nodded. "It all started right after Jonarka grabbed full control of the Vazakanian Empire and executed all the politicians that she couldn't buy with sponsorship. You see, Jonarka had convinced the people that their suffering was the government's fault. And, of course, Vazonya was the solution: Vazonya could give the people jobs if only the government wouldn't stand in the company's way." She shook her head. "People had no problem seeing the politicians die. Industry was deregulated to Jonarka's satisfaction, the government was replaced with Vazonya and she became the Queen."

"So did the resistance start because of that?" asked Jason.

"No," said Danya. "It started because Jonarka went beyond politicians and murdered the royal family too."

There was a pause as Danya took a bite of the Maluna.

"So, the murder of the royal family caused some people to question the Queen?" asked Jason.

"It shocked people," said Danya. "Many rumors came out of it. Some even said the Jonarka had spared a newborn child. And many people wanted to find that child. They got together to search, but over time, they began to protect anyone still loyal to the royal family."

Danya grabbed the Maluna and took another bite. Jason bit into his.

"Tastes like some sort of fruit," he said. He chewed and swallowed. "So what kinds of operations do you conduct out of this place?"

"I've got to train you before I can tell you anything," said Danya. "In the art of Kano-Vunto."

"Kano-what?" asked Jason.

"Kano-Vunto," said Danya. "A Vazakanian martial art: the deadliest style in the galaxy. All Ven Thar agents know it."

"What are Ven Thar agents?" asked Jason.

"The enemy," said Danya. "Jonarka's secret police force. You won't escape a Ven Thar agent alive if you don't know Kano-Vunto."

III: *The day was young as the child wandered through the halls in a blue hooded robe and a mask. All around, there were statues and exotic greenery along with jewel-encrusted fountains and murals.*

The child came to a set of wooden doors, pushing them open. Inside, there was a golden throne. It was vacant. The chamber was empty. The child turned and left the chamber, walking instead down another hallway that came to a dead end. The child stared at the end of the hallway for a moment. There was a statue to the left with sapphire eyes. The child placed a finger on both eyes of the statue.

The wall began to move. It slid open. The child stared at the sight.

[Come, young one,] said a woman in a similar blue hooded robe. She also wore a mask. [Your first sacrifice awaits,] she said.

The child walked into the chamber. The woman handed the child a sword. The child stepped up to the altar.

[Make me proud,] said the woman. [Show me that you can lead.]

The child pulled the sword up high, pausing for a moment to look down at the helpless man chained below. The child drove the sword down toward the throat of the man.

Queen Jonarka woke from her slumber as a man carrying a briefcase entered the royal chamber escorted by two guards. The man knelt before her.

[Your highness, we have carried out the test on project Yed Ven. I wish to discuss the results with you.]

[Excellent,] said the Queen. [Rise, Chairman. Guards, leave us.]

The guards inside the chamber all filed out of the chamber. The Chairman stood and opened the briefcase.

[The results were devastating,] he said. [The power of the new carrier design is superior to anything we've ever constructed, and certainly anything the Vonar brand has ever constructed.]

[Did they pass every trial?] asked the Queen.

[They could have passed more,] said the Chairman. [Easily. Watch this.]

The Queen looked on as the Chairman folded a screen out of the briefcase. A video of a massive warship firing on another massive warship began playing. After a moment, the second warship exploded.

[Excellent,] said the Queen. [We will proceed with the operation using your design. Your brand has won the contract. Yed Ven goes as planned, for Xiaf, and in the name of the Vazonian Empire. We will invade.]

[As you wish, your highness,] said the Chairman. [In the name of Xiaf.]

[You are dismissed,] said the Queen. [See to it that production unfolds without any problems. I wish to land a devastating blow to the heart of the Union.]

[Of course, your highness,] said the Chairman.

He bowed and then walked away.

The Queen pressed the button on the armrest of the throne. A man in a white robe with a blue sash walked into the royal chamber and bowed.

[You summoned me, your highness?] he asked.

[Kedán, has General Drefán arrived yet?] asked the Queen.

[He has, your highness,] said Kedán. [He awaits your company in the chamber.]

[Excellent,] said the Queen. [Xiaf will be pleased. Leave me. I must prepare myself.]

[At once, your highness,] said Kedán. He hurried out of the chamber and closed the door. The Queen stepped up to the altar.

[I am your servant,] she said. [Keep my spirit pure as I offer to you a sacrifice of rotted faith.]

The Queen bowed and stepped back, then leaving the chamber. She continued on through the palace and walked down a hallway, coming to a dead end. There was a statue of Xiaf on her left with sapphire eyes. The Queen put her fingers on the pair of eyes. The wall slid open to reveal an ancient chamber. General Drefán lay on the altar in a robe, chained there.

[I offer to Xiaf a sacrifice of a rotted soul,] said the Queen. [To keep me pure as I do what is bidden of me in your name.]

The Queen approached the General, drawing a sword from the hands of another statue.

IV: The Four-Star General stood in the Oval Office before the President of the United States.

"What exactly are you asking me, General Ulysses?" asked the President.

"We could make a statement to the rest of the Interstellar Union," said General Ulysses. "We could make this planet an invaluable asset to the Union simply by becoming the authority on military intelligence. I tell you, Mr. President, there is one thing we had right here in this country that no other star system in the Union has ever had, and that's a Cold War. We learned more about espionage and intelligence gathering during the Cold War than any of these other systems ever possibly could have. We may have nothing on the Vazonian Empire, but we're sure as hell closer to having something than anyone else in the Union. And we could use this to our advantage. The battlefront is drawing closer and closer to home everyday. If we can show the Union that we're an invaluable source of intelligence, then they will do everything they can to defend us from harm."

"You're sure that your theory is correct?" asked the President. "You're sure that we have a better understanding of intelligence gathering than they do?"

"It's not even close, Mr. President," said General Ulysses. "I'm asking you to put me in charge of the CIA. I will keep my position as General of the USPDF, but, with the CIA under my leadership, the now obscure government agency will become the most prominent source of interstellar intelligence in the Union. I promise you, sir."

The President paused. He nodded his head. "You have the job, General," said the President. "I reason that with the current state of the Central Intelligence Agency being somewhat irrelevant, replacing the current director with you gives us a very low risk with very high rewards."

"Thank you, Mr. President," said General Ulysses. "I promise you that this will be one of the best decisions you've ever made."

3:

I: Jason stood in the middle of the woods blindfolded as he listened carefully for movement. He was abruptly pushed to the ground on his chest and he felt a boot on his neck.

"You've got a lot to learn," said Danya. She removed her foot from his neck. He stood up and pulled his blindfold off. "What do they teach you?" she asked. "They even teach you defending yourself when you can't see?"

"Not like this," said Jason. "I'll learn. I'm noticing that this is a lot like Krav Maga. I do know some Krav Maga, but this takes it to another level."

"Try to kill me," said Danya. "Right now."

Jason stared at her. She looked him right in the eyes, her emerald gaze focused on him.

"Try to kill me," said Danya. "Show me what you can do."

Jason lunged at her. She caught him and redirected his momentum down to the ground. He rolled over as she went to step on his neck and he came to his feet. He abruptly stopped in his tracks and pointed behind her.

"What's that?" he asked.

Danya looked behind her. Jason pushed her down on her face and placed his foot on her neck in the way she just had on his.

"That probably would have done it," said Jason. "Weren't expecting that, were you?"

He lifted his boot off of her neck. She rose to her feet and brushed herself off.

"Might work once," she said. "But it'll never work again."

"Only needs to work once," said Jason. "I can fight. That move comes directly from Krav Maga."

"It was clever," said Danya. "Very clever. But it was very risky. The enemy can learn to look for it. And when it doesn't work, then what happens? Leaves you exposed, doesn't it? You have to learn moves that will work no matter what."

"You told me to try and kill you," said Jason. "You didn't say how." He nodded. "So job well done. What do I need to learn next?"

Danya had no trace of amusement on her face. "Just curious," she said. "You want to learn the right way, or do you want to die? The choice is yours."

Jason was silent.

"Agents don't tell you what they'll do to you before they do it," said Danya. She shook her head. "Agents will approach you silently. They'll get up close to you and you won't sense a thing." She stepped up right behind him. He could feel her breath on his neck. She spoke softly into his ear. "They'll get so close to you that you can feel the warmth of their body against yours, but, by then, it'll be too late: you'll be dead. They'll kill you."

"I see," said Jason. "I think I know enough not to let them get that close. I'm a soldier already. I'm not new to combat."

"You're naïve," said Danya. She stepped back in front of him and looked around the clearing, shaking her head. "Darkness is coming," she said. "You need to get up on time tomorrow."

Danya walked over to the trapdoor and pulled it open, climbing back down into the outpost. Jason followed her, closing the trapdoor behind them. Danya led him through the outpost and into their room. She took her boots off and climbed up onto her bed, sitting with her back to the wall as she grabbed a tattered book and opened it to a book marked page.

"Can I ask you something?" asked Jason.

"It would depend on what you ask," said Danya.

"It's about you," said Jason. "Personally."

"What do you want to know?" asked Danya.

"How did you get here?" asked Jason. "Where did you come from?"

"I defected to the resistance with Grand General Sazún," said Danya. "He took me in after his brother died and he taught me to fight."

"Do you have a family?" asked Jason.

"All executed by Ven Thar," said Danya. "Suspicion of crimes against Xiaf. And Ven Thar wasn't wrong about the suspicion. All of my family still followed the Vazakanian Way and the Vazakanian Lifestyle."

"What's the Vazakanian Way?" asked Jason.

"People followed it before Jonarka foced them to follow Xiaf," said Danya. "Not quite a religion, but definitely a philosophy, it was about having a balanced mind: a balance of thought and instinct."

"Why can't that philosophy work with faith in Xiaf?" asked Jason.

"Xiaf commands loyalty and obedience," said Danya. "Faith in Xiaf frees you of thought and represses instinct. If you do as Xiaf commands, you have nothing to worry about. This all rose out of a business model. What better way is there to appeal to people than to captivate them spiritually? If you captivate the people spiritually, you have absolute power over them."

"What do you mean?" asked Jason.

"Thought is dangerous," said Danya. "Instinct is dangerous. If people think about what's right and wrong or trust their instincts when thought can't give them a clear answer, then Xiaf has no power."

"Why does Xiaf have no power if that happens?" asked Jason.

"Because if you believe in Xiaf, then you believe that people can't solve their own problems," said Danya. "You need Xiaf to guide you to happiness. To accept Xiaf is to believe that humanity is incapable of survival without divine guidance. Xiaf is a deity that asks for blind faith. The Vazakanian Way opens one's eyes."

II: The Queen dropped the sword on the altar next to the lifeless body of the General. She walked out of the chamber. Kedán stood there.

[Was the sacrifice successful, your highness?] he asked.

[It was,] said the Queen. [Xaif will be pleased with my work. We are blessed with good fortune for many days to come.] The Queen paused. She looked at a statue of Xiaf and then looked back at Kedán.

[My only fear, Kedán, is what the future beyond the present will hold. In my mind, I now see a dark future for the blessings we're given. I worry that the sacrifice could be losing its power each day.]

[What do you mean, your highness?] asked Kedán. [How could the sacrifice possibly be losing its power?]

[It does not feel as it once did with the power of Xiaf filling my body,] said the Queen. [It has become a struggle.]

Kedán paused. [What could be done about this?] he asked.

[Bring me the man named Faustemi from the world of Goletem,] said the Queen. [That is what I ask of you. Bring me the one they call the healer.]

[What do you seek from this man?] asked Kedán.

[A favor,] said the Queen. She began walking through the palace. Kedán followed her. [I seek revival,] said the Queen.

The Queen entered the royal chamber once more and took her seat on the throne. She closed her eyes. The moments passed by as she fell asleep.

The child stood by the beverage table in the ballroom. The masked woman walked up to the child, followed by a second and much taller figure wearing a blue hooded robe and a mask just as the child and the woman did. Next to the taller figure was a shorter figure, also dressed in a blue hooded robe and a mask.

[Young one,] said the masked woman. [I would like to introduce you to the Director and Grand General Nu Kufán Vih Sensán.]

The child looked up into the mask of the Director.

[Adorable,] said the Director. [In time, you'll grow into a fine ruler of an empire.]

There was a commotion in the crowd. The sound of footsteps echoed out across the floor. A man wielding a firearm stepped before the child.

A gunshot echoed through the ballroom. The man with the firearm held his hand to his chest as a nearby guard stepped forward with a rifle aimed at him. The Director jumped forward and threw the man face down on the floor, then unsheathing a sword from the guard.

[Young one,] said the Director. [This man has betrayed us. What have you learned to do to those who betray us?]

The Director handed the child the sword. The Director stepped down on the wounded man's back. The child lifted the sword up high, brining it down forcefully once again.

III: Director General Ulysses placed his nametag on his new desk. He then took a yellow piece of paper from a notepad and walked down the hallway with it, stepping up to the conference room and tacking it to the door there before stepping inside and looking down at his watch. A moment passed and there was a knock on the door. The Director rose from the seat and opened it. Two men stood behind the door.

"Welcome, gentlemen," said Ulysses. "I see you figured it out."

Two more men and a woman walked up to the doorway.

"Anyone else coming?" asked Ulysses. "Anyone else follow the clues I left them?"

"Who are you?" asked the woman.

"Director General Henry Ulysses," said the Director. "I'm now in charge of the CIA. And what we're going to do is to turn this agency into the most prominent source of interstellar intelligence in the galaxy."

Three more men and another woman entered the room.

"If one of you will please lock the door, I would like to begin outlining the new mission statement of the Central Intelligence Agency," said Ulysses. "Everyone who did not follow the clues to meet here is fired. A true member of an intelligence department would never ignore signs they've never seen before. So the nine of you and myself will now assume all major roles in running this agency. Should those who I've fired wish to come back, they will need to be retrained in the art of intelligence gathering and they will be forced to work their way back into this building. Are there any questions so far?"

No one said anything.

"I find it hard to believe that intelligence officers would have no questions," said Ulysses. "Never be afraid to ask questions."

"Why weren't we informed of the fact that there would be a change at your position?" asked one of the women.

"Because our enemies won't tell us what they're going to do to us before they do it," said Ulysses. "And it's our job as an intelligence agency to figure things out before they happen. Any other questions?"

"What experience do you have?" asked one of the men.

"I'm also in charge of the United States Planetary Defense Force," said Ulysses. "I, however, am now determined to make this very agency the primary source of intelligence for the entire Interstellar Union. Eventually, we will rival the Vazonian Ven Thar in intelligence gathering ability."

"What makes us qualified to do this?" asked the first woman.

"What's your name, ma'am?" asked the Director.

"Harmony," said Harmony. "Harmony Chance."

"Well, Harmony, the rest of the Interstellar Union never had a Cold War," said Ulysses. "They never had a war that was waged purely through espionage and nothing more than that. In fact, very few civilizations ever have. Our experience in intelligence gathering is far superior to anything that anyone else could offer. This is our mission, ladies and gentlemen. Under my leadership, we will turn the tide of this war in our favor."

IV:

General Kufán walked down the street in his civilian clothes. He looked around and continued down an alleyway to a worn metal door. He knocked three times.

[Password?] asked a voice on the other side.

[Plitano,] said Kufán.

The door opened. A second man wearing a traditional Vazakanian black robe looked at the General.

[Who are you?] asked the man. [What do you want?]

[I have information about Vazonian military operations that I would like to trade for my freedom,] said the General.

[Enter,] said the second man. He allowed the General to enter. It was a kitchen. The second man led the General to a back room and closed the door. Two women were inside. They were both wearing traditional Vazakanian white robes with white sashes.

[Search him,] said the man.

One of the women stepped forward and began to feel around the General's body.

[He's clean,] she said.

[I can take no more of the humiliation I face,] said Kufán. [I wish to defect to the resistance.]

[And why would the resistance want you?] asked the second man. [We know who you are. The blood of innumerable patriots is on your hands. What information could you give us in return for your safety?]

[What do you want to know?] asked Kufán. [I know many things.]

[Locations of secret Vazonian facilities are very useful to us,] said the second man. [Would you know the location of any facilities we might wish to know about?]

[San Tun Zaf,] said the General. [The highest-level detainment facility there is. I can tell you where it is. But I will only do so once I'm safely under your protection.]

The second man said nothing for a moment. [You have a deal,] he said. We will arrange to transport you immediately. The second man reached into a desk drawer and took out a small communication device. He gave it to the General. [Use this to contact us,] he said. He looked at the two women in the room. [Sisters, please escort the General back outside and send a courier to contact Grand General Sazún. A defector with a profile this high must be handled with extra caution.]

4:

I: Jason stumbled over the root of a tree as he struggled to navigate his way back to the outpost. Both of the planet's crescent moons shone brightly in the sky behind the canopy of the trees overhead.

Jason stopped walking and looked around, trying to get his bearings in what little light shone through the trees. He was lost in the woods. He took out his communicator.

"I'm lost," he said. "I have no idea where I am."

He waited. There was no response. He repeated himself. Again, there was no response. He felt the communicator in his hands. It had no power pack. He cursed under his breath and took a look around again, trying to make out anything that looked familiar.

II: Danya sat underground in the outpost with a timer in her hands. General Hatshenya walked up behind her.

[He hasn't called for help?] asked Hatshenya.

[The communicator I gave him has no power pack,] said Danya. [He's probably called for help many times.]

[Are you trying to teach him or are you trying to be cruel to him?] asked Hatshenya. [I struggle to understand your thinking sometimes. Your teaching methods often border on the edge of brutality.]

[Trying to humble him,] said Danya. She nodded. [He thinks he already knows everything he needs to know. There's only one way to show him he doesn't.]

[There are many dangers in the forest,] said Hatshenya. [Dangers he doesn't know.]

[He knows them now,] said Danya. [He'll make it back.]

[I hope you're right,] said Hatshenya.

III:

The Queen looked down at the masked man.

[What do ask of me, your highness?] he asked.

[What I ask of you, Faustemi, is simple,] said the Queen. She paused. [I ask you for the gift of revival.]

Faustemi was silent.

[It is my understanding that you can grant me my wish,] said the Queen. [That you could revive me to the youth I once had.]

[In what way do you mean, your highness?] asked Faustemi.

[In order to maintain the blessing of Xiaf for the empire, I must make sacrifices,] said the Queen. [But now that I have aged, the toll they take on my body makes me fear for the future of the empire. I ask you, humbly, to give me the gift of youth.]

[I do not believe that even with all of the empire's resources,] said Faustemi, [that anyone could be given the gift of immortality.]

[I am confident that you can make it happen,] said the Queen. [You will go to work immediately.]

Faustemi was silent.

[Immediately,] said the Queen. [You are dismissed.]

Faustemi left the chamber.

IV: Ulysses sat at the head of the table.

"This is what we know about our enemy," he said. "We know that their leader is a woman named Jonarka and we know that they fanatically follow a religion with a deity called Xiaf. We know that their technology is far more advanced than anything we have, and we know that they will destroy us if we do not submit to them and convert to their faith. We know that Jonarka's secret police force is called Ven Thar, and it gives her the power she has. That, ladies and gentlemen, is all we know. The first order of business for us as the new Central Intelligence Agency will be for everyone to learn their customs and their language."

"What purpose will this serve, sir?" asked Harmony.

"It will give us a better understanding of our enemy," said Ulysses. "How they think. Once we understand how they think, then we can begin to carry out intelligence gathering operations in their territory. So ladies and gentlemen: cenaski. That's how you say hello in the Vazonian language. Say it."

"Cenaski," said the people at the table.

"Good," said Ulysses. "We'll be speaking their language in no time."

V:
Jason listened carefully. He could hear rushing water. He looked as hard as he could into the darkness. He saw the clearing. He walked into it and lifted the trapdoor, climbing down into the outpost and closing the trapdoor behind him. He found Danya waiting for him.

"Time," she said. She shrugged her shoulders. "Timer ran out of battery. You took a while out there. I thought you already knew enough not to need the training."

"Is that what this was all about?" asked Jason. "Well, you've made your point. I don't know anything."

"Are you sure?" asked Danya. "You know nothing?"

"Nothing," said Jason. "Now can I please go to bed?"

Danya rose from the chair and stepped out of his way. He began walking through the outpost. Danya could be heard behind him. He walked into their room and lay down in bed. He closed his eyes and fell asleep.

VI:
Zerpanya carefully adjusted the focusing motors in her electronic eye. She heard footsteps in the hallway. She snapped the cover of the eye back into place and stood up. A uniformed man took a look at her.

[I apologize, Director,] he said. [You had your door open. I did not realize you weren't decent.]

[Think nothing of it, General Blayán,] said Zerpanya. [I have no shame in my eye. Living with an electronic eye has hardened me as a person.] She paused. [Why have you come to my quarters?]

[We must speak of this privately,] said Blayán. He stepped inside and closed the door. [I fear that General Kufán has become an informant to the resistance.]

[He wouldn't dare,] said Zerpanya. [He doesn't have the strength of will to commit an act of treason.]

[I fear that he does,] said Blayán. [I ask your permission to monitor his actions.]

[What leads you to believe this, General?] asked Zerpanya. [What evidence is there?]

[General Kufán has been heard speaking quietly in his quarters while no one else is present inside,] said Blayán. [And several days ago, he abruptly disappeared from the base without any explanation.]

[I grant you permission to monitor him then,] said Zerpanya. [If he has committed treason, I must know so I may deal with him personally.]

[Of course, Director,] said Blayán. [I will begin at once.] He nodded. [And one other matter, Director. I believe we've uncovered new evidence as to where the resistance outpost could be.]

[What evidence do you speak of?] asked Zerpanya.

[Near the crash site, footprints lead deep into the forest along the mountain river,] said Blayán. [What if the outpost is along the river somewhere?]

[Such a location would be very sensible,] said Zerpanya. [Send out an expedition team to survey the area along the mountain river. Perhaps this could lead us to the outpost.]

VII:

Jason woke up to the sound of an alarm. He shot up in bed and looked around the room. There was a small timing device with a note attached to it on Danya's bed. He walked over to it and shut the alarm off, looking down at the note. 'Come find me,' it said.

Jason put his boots on and left the room, walking to the dining area and looking around. As usual, there were a number of other people there, laughing and talking and playing their card games. But Danya wasn't there. At the table they usually sat at, however, there was a young woman dressed in the exact same two-piece outfit that Danya wore. This woman's sash, however, was purple rather than grey. Jason went over to her.

"Hello," he said. "My name is Jason. What do you call yourself?"

"Sabenya," said Sabenya. "Nice to meet you."

"Are you Vazakanian?" asked Jason.

"Proudly," said Sabenya. She smiled. "How did you know?"

"I suppose it would be the way you dress," said Jason. "Danya dresses the same way. And she's told me she's Vazakanian, so it seems to be the most logical conclusion." Jason nodded. "I found it hard to understand the way she dresses, but now that I see another Vazakanian dressed the same way, I would assume it's just customary for your people, isn't it?"

"The outfit is called a libranya," said Sabenya. "For over seven thousand five hundred years, women wore this in my culture. Here in the resistance, Vazakanian women proudly keep the tradition alive."

"It captivates a man's attention," said Jason. "If you get what I'm saying."

"It's a part of embracing the Vazakanian Lifestyle," said Sabenya. She smiled. "In our culture, we have pride in the body nature gave us. It's a liberation from shame. We're not ashamed of our bodies."

"Danya said nothing about this when she told me about the Vazakanian Way," said Jason.

"Well, this isn't a part of the Vazakanian Way," said Sabenya. "This is part of the Vazakanian Lifestyle. There's a difference between the two. You can follow the Vazakanian Way without embracing the lifestyle. The way doesn't dictate the lifestyle."

"I see," said Jason. He nodded and looked around the room again. "So do you have any idea where Danya might be?"

"I've known Danya longer than just about everyone in the resistance," said Sabenya. "But she's not very much like a Vazakanian."

"I get the sense that she's not very much like anything," said Jason. "She seems like a robot: cold, lacking in personality, and so far, I haven't seen her laugh or smile once."

"She won't show emotion," said Sabenya. "She's the most dangerous fighter we have. If she even feels emotion, she never shows it."

"I was beginning to believe all Vazakanians were just like her," said Jason.

"You will never meet any other Vazakanians like her," said Sabenya. "Vazakanians are a very proud and jovial people. She's proud, but never jovial."

"Why is she different?" asked Jason.

"No one knows," said Sabenya. "We know she's lived a hard life, but no one knows anything about it beyond that."

There was a pause.

"Why are you sitting here by yourself?" asked Jason.

"I was about to leave," said Sabenya. She rose from her seat and walked away. Jason stepped up and looked where she'd been seated. There was a note on the floor there. Jason grabbed the note and walked up to Sabenya with it.

"What does this say?" he asked.

"I can't read or write," said Sabenya. "I apologize."

Jason paused for a moment but then walked out of the dining area and went back to the room. He picked up the tattered book he always saw Danya reading and opened it to the book marked page. There was another note. There were a number of scribbles, each with an English letter next to it. It was a translation key. He stared at both notes for a moment.

"In the cave," he said. He left the room once more and began walking through the base. He came to the elevator he'd been pushed into when he'd first been taken into the outpost. He stepped on it and pressed a button. Nothing happened. He pressed another button. The elevator began rising.

He found himself in total darkness. He took one step forward and then he was knocked to the ground. He felt a boot over his neck.

"Not bad," said Danya. "But you always need to be ready to fight. When the situation is uncertain, always be ready to fight. You understand me?"

"I do now," said Jason. He pasued. "And I figured something like this would happen too."

"So what did you just learn?" asked Danya. "What's the lesson?"

"When I don't know what to expect, I need to be ready to defend myself," said Jason. "I think."

Danya nodded. "You found me surprisingly fast," she said. "Good work."

"So what's next?" asked Jason.

"Simple," said Danya. "I need to teach you the Kano-Vunto fighting style."

"You going to take your foot off of my neck?" asked Jason.

Danya paused. "Of course," she said. She removed her foot from his neck and he stood up. Danya shone a light on the elevator pad and stepped onto it. Jason did the same. It lowered them back into the base. "Back to the woods," said Danya. "You'll need to listen this time."

"I understand," said Jason. "I'll listen."

5:

I: Ulysses stood in the conference room holding a script in his hands. Harmony stood before him with a script in her own hands.

"Cenaski, Zidonya," said General Ulysses. "Jyaski besha vu?"

"Zha bema sotanya," said Harmony. "Du vu?"

"Zha bema sotán nu lokwán," said General Ulysses. He turned to the other people in the conference room. "This is how their language sounds. All ten of us will have the ability to speak, read, write, and understand their language just as fluently as they can in time." He paused. "Has everyone here memorized their alphabet? Raise your hand if you have."

Everyone raised their hands.

"So let's have a little review then," said Ulysses. He took a marker and wrote a series of symbols on the board. "What does it say?" he asked.

The room was silent.

"Elephant," said Harmony. "Spelled with an F."

"Good job, Harmony," said General Ulysses. "We will all learn to instantly identify what the written language says, and once we do that, we will learn what it means. But for now, we will be learning transliterated Vazonian. Are there any questions? Peter?"

"Are we going to be working with anyone that actually speaks the language?" asked Peter. "An actual Vazonian maybe? One that's on our side?"

"We're working on figuring out, first, what percentage of Vazonians, if there is one, are dissenters of the Vazonian Empire," said Ulysses. "We're certain that there must be some people in the Vazonian Empire that disagree with the Queen, but finding them is the problem."

"Does the Interstellar Union ever receive any defectors?" asked Harmony.

"No," said Ulysses. "Which puzzles us. There has never been a single one."

"Why do we think that is?" asked Peter. "Any theories?"

"None that make any sense," said Ulysses. "I refuse to believe that the Vazonian Empire could have stopped every single potential defector over the last two decades. It's now been twenty-one years since the Vazonian Empire declared war on the Interstellar Union. The Queen conquers a planet, offers the people Xiaf, and then sacrifices those who don't take the offer."

"What if the defectors are defecting to somewhere else?" asked Peter.

"What do you mean, Peter?" asked Ulysses. "Where else would they defect to?"

"Think about this, sir," said Peter. "If those are the Queen's methods, then she must alienate a lot of people. What if these people have organized themselves into a resistance?"

Ulysses was silent for a moment. "Intriguing," he said. "That no one in the Interstellar Union could have ever come up with such a theory. You could be right, Peter. There very well could be a resistance force or forces in the Vazonian Empire. And if we were to find proof that one or more exist, then the intelligence community would notice us. What a breakthrough it would be."

"Maybe this should be our first objective, sir," said Peter.

II: Faustemi cycled to the next slide. He examined the scar tissue and took notes in his notebook.

[The possibility simply isn't there,] he said. [It is the progression of nature to age and to lose the endurance of youth.]

[You must never speak of nature before the Queen,] said the assistant. [It is sacrilege in the eyes of Xiaf.]

[I must think more of this,] said Faustemi. [The things I have done to give people new life, and the things I have done to heal those on the edge of death; but how does one heal that which is in perfect health? I must read the literature. Konsel, close down the laboratory. I must ask the Queen's permission to access the forbidden library.]

[The forbidden library?] asked Konsel. [What could be found to help your research in the texts shunned by Xiaf?]

[We shall see,] said Faustemi. [Perhaps there may be another way.]

Faustemi left the laboratory.

III: Jason stood crouched in his fighter's stance as he waited for the attack. Danya threw her right palm up toward his nose. She stopped her hand just before it hit his nose.

"Breaks your nose and drives your broken nose up into your brain," said Danya, "killing you. Now, how do you defend against it? I'll go in slow motion."

Jason assumed his fighter stance again and Danya slowly went into the lethal motion. Jason pivoted his body sideways and grabbed her arm, carrying the arc of her momentum downward into the ground. She now lay on her back.

"Wrong," said Danya. "I need to fall on my front: always on the front."

"Why?" asked Jason.

"On your back, you can still move your arms and legs," said Danya. "On your front, you can't move them nearly as much."

"I see," said Jason. "So how do I counter that move correctly then?"

"Grab and push down," said Danya. "That's always your goal: put the enemy face down on the ground. You understand that?"

"Makes sense," said Jason. "A lot of sense, actually."

"It's never going to be that simple though," said Danya. "Ven Thar agents have guns."

Danya drew her pistol and pointed it at Jason. "What do you do?" she asked.

"What can I do?" asked Jason. "Surrender."

"No," said Danya. "A bullet: how big is a bullet from a handgun?"

"Pretty small," said Jason. "Compared to your body."

"Then think," said Danya. "You have your chest exposed to me. Turn your body sideways."

Jason turned sideways.

"Wrong side," said Danya. "The left side of the body has the heart. Always turn your right side toward the enemy. Pivot, grab the wrist and the weapon, and push me face down to the ground while you wrench the gun away."

Danya holstered her weapon. "Ready?" she asked. "Try it."

She went to draw the pistol and Jason turned sideways, grabbing the weapon and her wrist as he wrenched the gun out of her hand. He pushed her down to the ground.

"Good," said Danya. "Still won't help you much though. Most often, you'll find a gun pointed at you before you realize it. And when that happens, you're in trouble unless you know exactly what to do."

"How do I get out of a situation like that?" asked Jason.

Danya handed the pistol to Jason. She looked him right in the eyes. "Point it at me," she said. "Like you're going to kill me." Jason pointed it at her. She put her hands up. Her expression changed. "I surrender," she said. She paused. "Now try to cuff me. What would you do if you had handcuffs?"

Jason stepped up to her. In one quick motion, she wrenched the gun out of his hand and pointed it at him. "Takes a lot of practice," she said. "Try it."

Jason raised his hands. "I surrender," he said. He waited as Danya stepped up to him to cuff him. He made his move. It failed.

"Wrong," said Danya. "Not going to work. You have to be quick. You need to have perfect hand-eye coordination."

Danya pointed the gun at Jason again. Again, he put his hands up. Danya went to cuff him. He lunged at her, struggling with her to the ground and finally managing to get the gun away from her.

"Needs practice," she said. "Lots of practice. This is what we're going to work on for the rest of the day."

IV: General Kufán locked the door to his office and opened his desk drawer, removing a panel at the bottom of the drawer. He took out the radio device. He turned it on.

[Hello,] he said. [Is anyone there?]

[Password?] asked the device.

"Maluna," said the General.

[What is your status?] asked the speaker.

[I must come to you now,] said the General. [I will meet you at point Ben Sen. Do I have your word that you will protect me?]

[You have our word,] said the communicator. [You will be substantially rewarded and we will give you our full protection as long as you continue to tell us what we want to know.]

[I will tell you everything,] said the General. [But I will tell you nothing more at this point. I will meet you at the Ben Zen point. End transmission.]

General Kufán put the device back in the drawer and left his office. He walked through the facility toward the hangar. He arrived at the entrance and found an armed squad of soldiers there along with General Blayán.

[Hello, General Kufán,] said Blayán. [We would love to accompany you. Come aboard. Take us to your destination.]

General Kufán looked at the group of men for a moment, but then stepped forward.

V: General Kufán sat at the controls of the spacecraft. All was silent.

[Piece of filth,] said General Blayán. [You will die the death of a traitor in the eyes of Xiaf.]

General Blayán left the cockpit and went back into the cabin. As this happened, Kufán quietly reached into his left pocket. He pulled his hand out and sat back in the chair. He then flipped his thumb up and a large blade surged out of his hand. The General swung his arm around and slashed the throat of the guard on his left. The guard dropped his weapon and Kufán caught his gun, taking it and knocking the second guard on the forehead with its stock, denting his skull. Kufán leapt to his feet and fired the weapon, taking everyone else in the cockpit down. The door to the cockpit opened and three more guards rushed in. Kufán took two of them down, but the third got to him and wrestled him to the floor. Kufán reached across the floor and grabbed a hold of the knife. He plunged it into the guard's neck and threw the guard away, picking up another gun and exiting the cockpit. He went into the cabin and pointed the gun at General Blayán.

[Into the closet,] said Kufán. [Now.]

[You piece of filth,] said Blayán. [I'd sooner die than take orders from you.]

Kufán fired a round into Blayán's shoulder. Blayán cried out in pain and then stood up and ran at Kufán. Kufán took the stock of the weapon and clubbed Blayán on the head with it. Kufán pulled the other general up and pushed him inside the closet, locking it and heading to the cockpit. He worked the controls for a moment and then sat down on the pilot's chair. The craft changed its course. The moments passed by and the vessel came to an island in the ocean. There was a second spacecraft there. The General landed the craft.

VI: Director Zerpanya stepped down onto the floor of the hangar. A young lieutenant raced up to her and saluted.

[Director,] he said. [General Blayán has not returned. Was he to be gone this long?]

The Director paused for a moment. [He was not to be gone at all,] she said. [Why did he leave?]

[He informed us that he would be taking a short flight with General Kufán,] said the lieutenant. [Neither has returned.]

[The filth,] said Zerpanya. [Come, lieutenant, let us go to the command center to see where they were going.]

[Yes, Director,] said the lieutenant. He began following the Director through the base. They came to the command center.

[Access the emergency location transmitter of the vessel they took,] said Zerpanya. [Tell me where it is.]

The lieutenant took a moment to carry out the order. [Shifou Island, Director,] he said. [Due east in the ocean.]

[Thank you, lieutenant,] said Zerpanya.

She turned and walked away, heading through the base to the armory where she armed herself with a large pistol. She then went back to the hangar and prepared a vessel for takeoff. After a short time, she piloted the craft up into the air and it began charging over the terrain of the planet. As the autopilot took over, Zerpanya looked down at the weapon she had chosen. She armed it.

The island came into view. The missing spacecraft was on the beach. Zerpanya landed her craft and left it, walking briskly up the boarding ramp of the other vessel and finding a sight of carnage. None of the bodies belonged to General Kufán.

A sound came from the closet. Zerpanya leveled her weapon and threw the door open. It was General Blayán.

[The traitor filth,] he said. [We did not search him before we took him prisoner.] The General held his arm where he had been shot. [I could hear a second craft taking off once he landed.]

[No Kasanosi,] said Zerpanya. [This is one of their signature tactics in moving personnel.]

The General brought himself to his feet. [We must inform the Queen,] he said. [If General Kufán has defected, we can only assume that he will tell them everything he knows.]

[And I thought he lacked the courage,] said Zerpanya. [Very well. If he would like to die a traitor, then we will grant him his wish.]

VII: Jason stood blindfolded as he sensed his

surroundings. He caught Danya and directed her down to the ground. He placed his foot over her throat and took his blindfold off.

"Good," said Danya. She climbed back to her feet. Jason saw the move. She reached for her pistol. He turned sideways and correctly took the gun from her, pushing her down on the ground.

"Excellent," said Danya. "You had no warning and you defended yourself. Very good." She climbed to her feet again. "You've learned all you need to know. Tomorrow, we'll begin your routine training drills."

Danya lifted the trapdoor and descended down into the outpost. Jason followed her. They made their way through the base and into their room. Jason lay down on his bed and watched as Danya removed her pistol from its holster and sat down on the side of her bed as she examined it carefully.

She holstered the weapon and took the loose ends of the sash that held her top closed in her hands. She began to pull. It was tied like one would tie a shoelace. He stared at her where he lay, watching as she pulled the knot apart, the front of the top she wore sliding open, but not enough to reveal what lay beneath it.

Jason opened his mouth as if to say something, but then he closed it and continued to stare as she stretched her arms over her head and then leaned back on her hands for a moment, stretching her legs. The front of the top fell open completely. Jason took in the sight, his gaze falling upon her breasts: large and round with a slight comforting sag to their shape as they hung bare before his eyes, so elegant, and with such beauty that he'd never seen before in a woman. She paused for a moment, oblivious to his interest, and then went about removing the holster from the sash and then removing the sash from the top entirely.

She looked over her body and widened the stance of her thighs where she sat, stretching them as far apart as they could go. He looked downward as she did so, staring in shock. It had not been apparent to him that she wore nothing beneath her skirt. He eyed the vertical seam of her feminine flesh as she sat on the bed: a pleasant view of a sensual rift: smooth as silk all around, but parted loosely by two lobes of wrinkled pink subtlety from within, each falling buried deep beneath a hooded cusp wound gently around at the top as if sculpted from a block of harmonious intrigue as she finally noticed the look in his eyes and nodded her head at him from where she sat. She had not a single hair anywhere on her body save for her head and it didn't look as if there ever had been any in her life. She was more beautiful than any woman Jason had ever seen. He leveled his gaze with hers, putting forth his best effort to keep it there, but he found the task impossible.

"You seeing something you've never seen before?" asked Danya. "Would you like a picture?"

"I'd be lying if I said no," said Jason. "I'd frame the picture if I could have one. I've never seen a body like yours. To see such beauty in a place so dirty: it's very comforting. I mean that as a sincere compliment from a man to a woman."

"Spare me," said Danya. "Please. I may be Vazakanian, but I say that if we could be a whole lot more focused on the resistance, then we'd be unstoppable."

"Is that what you believe?" asked Jason. "That's a shame."

"What's the point?" asked Danya. "Our lives are in danger. We don't need distractions."

"Then can I ask you something?" asked Jason.

"If it's a question worth answering," said Danya. She closed the stance of her inner thighs. Now only her breasts were exposed to view.

"What do you plan on doing once you overthrow the Vazonian Empire?" asked Jason. "What will your people do?"

Danya rose from the bed and walked over to a dresser in the corner of the room. She opened the top drawer and took out a second grey sash. It was a darker shade of the color than the one she had just removed. She threaded it through her top and the holster and tied it in place there beneath her breasts.

"We'll have to write a new constitution," she said. "Elect new leaders, try to pick up the pieces left by the Queen. It'll take a lot of work."

"And what will you, yourself, do?" asked Jason. "Where will you go? What are your personal dreams?"

"Me?" asked Danya. She paused. "I don't think about it. I take every day as it comes to me."

"Well, I ask because, from what I've seen of you so far," said Jason. "I can't imagine you doing anything other than fighting."

Danya was silent.

"It's as if you're focused entirely on fighting and on nothing else beyond that," said Jason. "That's all you do and that's all you want to do."

"What else do you expect me to do?" asked Danya. "There's no time for anything else in war."

"I see other people here making time for other things," said Jason. "In the dining area, they laugh and tell jokes, they socialize, and they play card games. But for you, there's nothing but fighting and training. It's almost like you're afraid of getting to know people."

"Just get some rest," said Danya. "Less talk and more sleep. You need to wake up on time tomorrow."

VIII: Director Zerpanya studied the image before her. She cycled to the next image. There was nothing. It was yet another snow-covered mountain. A general walked up to her. She turned and looked down at him.

[Director, we've found the outpost near the crash site,] he said. [It appears that the pilot walked through the woods and found it for us.]

[Excellent,] said Zerpanya. [We will raid it immediately. Where is it?]

[In a cave just beneath a waterfall along the river in the area,] said the General. [We followed the pilot's tracks and found it. There are multiple exits. We've diagramed them for you already.]

[Good work, General,] said Zerpanya. [Sound the alarm. There's no time to waste. The information we gather at this outpost could lead us right to the base.]

[Indeed, it could,] said the General. [We must put our best soldiers on this mission.]

[Yes,] said Zerpanya. [I will personally lead it myself.]

[Director, I admire your courage,] said the General, [But, by Xiaf, the empire could not possibly afford for you be harmed.]

[I can take care of myself, General,] said Zerpanya. [I will lead the mission. I will make sure that we succeed. Now scramble the troops.]

[Yes, Director,] said the General. He walked over to a red button behind a glass case and pressed it. An alarm began to sound through the base.

Zerpanya made her way down into the assembly area.

6:

I: Danya snapped awake as a loud klaxon blared inside the room. She leapt to her feet and grabbed an assault rifle from beneath her bed. She looked at Jason.

"Time to fight," she said. "Get up."

Danya threw a second assault rifle to Jason and he caught it. Danya quickly stepped into her boots. Jason stepped into his own boots and followed Danya as she went down the hallway knocking on doors and calling for an evacuation. Jason followed her through the complex. The ground began to shake around them and loud blasts echoed through the halls. Danya led Jason to a ladder. She pressed a button on the wall and a door opened above the ladder. She went up first, finding a ring of armed guards waiting there.

Danya dropped both the assault rifle and the pistol from her holster and put her hands up. Another woman stepped through the crowd. She smiled as Jason climbed up. The woman looked at Jason.

"I've found you," she said. She spoke English. "We've been looking all over for you. Thank you for leading us to this outpost."

The woman stepped in front of Danya. The woman looked down at her for a moment. "I know you from somewhere," said the woman. The woman was silent for another moment. "No," she said. "It can't be." She stared for a moment more and nodded her head. "Remarkable," she said. "I don't believe this: Danya, my darling, you're alive. It was thought to be impossible. Do you remember me?"

"I don't remember the Queen's pawns," said Danya. "It's too hard to tell you apart. There's something wrong with your eye though."

"Quite the attitude you have," said the woman. "We'll see how that attitude changes at San Tun Zaf."

"Says who?" asked Danya. "What's your name?"

"My name?" asked the woman. "Director Na Zerpanya Vih Yedenya. You were twelve years old when we met if I'm correct. You had it all, Danya. You could have lived a happy life, but you gave it all away. This is the life you chose." The woman looked down at Danya. The woman was very tall. "I remember you kissed me once and called me your aunt. How about giving me a kiss for old time sake?"

The woman kissed Danya. Danya threw her head against the woman's skull as it happened, knocking her over as Danya kicked her pistol up off the ground and back into her hand. She pointed the gun at the woman's head, holding her in a headlock as she did so. Immediately, one of the other armed guards put a gun to Jason's head.

Danya backed away with Zerpanya, stepping down into the outpost. Once she had descended deep enough, she threw Zerpanya to the ground and ran to the second hangar. General Hatshenya was already preparing the craft for takeoff with Sabenya and a man Danya had never seen before. He was dressed in a Vazonian uniform.

"They've sealed all the exits," said Danya. "We have to get out of here."

Danya raced over to the computer terminal and input a clearance code. She quickly selected the correct function and confirmed it. The console began counting down in Vazakanian numerals as a second alarm began to sound. Danya raced into the spacecraft and it lifted off the ground as the computer console erupted into flames. The craft broke through the tree canopy and lifted off into space.

II:

"The Vazonian Empire emerged out of what was once known as the Vazakanian Empire," said Ulysses. "The Vazakanian Empire was a civilization founded on a very different ideology from what we find in the Vazonian Empire. For over seven thousand five hundred Vazakanian years, essentially the same number of Earth years, the Vazakanian people lived in prosperity with the ideology of the Vazakanian Way. They were not religious, but they believed strongly in the purity of nature. Idealistically, they believed that balance was the key to health and happiness. The balanced state of mind was a balance between thought and instinct. With our own civilization founded on Judeo-Christian ideology, we would find the Vazakanian lifestyle somewhat shocking. The first article of the original Vazakanian constitution gave every Vazakanian citizen the right to freedom of sexuality. That's right, ladies and gentlemen: I said the right to freedom of sexuality. Before the rise of the empire's Queen Vazakanya, much of the world considered women to be slaves in a world ruled by men. The sexual freedom article was the Queen's way of telling the women of the world that they no longer had to do what men asked of them: they were free to do whatever they pleased."

"So wait a minute," said Peter. "You're telling us that the first article of their constitution allowed them to do whatever the hell they wanted to sexually?"

"It was a different culture from ours, Peter," said Ulysses. "Different customs work in different cultures."

"But I don't even want to think of some of the things that must have gone on there with that article," said Peter.

"They were a very peaceful and prosperous civilization for over thirty times longer than we've been around," said Ulysses. "Let's not be ethnocentric, people. This article of the constitution ushered in a golden age for their civilization. Their tourism industry was the most vibrant in the entire galaxy for millennia. But then only three decades ago now, a catastrophic volcano eruption on the Vazakanian agricultural center, Nobanya, devastated the economy. There was a disease that they could not find a cure for, there was poverty, there was an inept and corrupt government, and their once vibrant tourism industry sharply declined due in large part to widespread fear of disease and violence. That was when Jonarka began to sponsor their politicians and preach faith in Xiaf as the way to salvation. She rose to power and now her corporation controls more than half of the galaxy. Her empire is run like a business. While it may seem on the surface like there is no free enterprise, the company has thousands and thousands of different brands all competing for contracts with the parent company. It is a very unusual model for the governance of an empire. Jonarka believes firmly that government is inherently evil and that the will of industry should govern her people."

"But she's an autocratic dictator," said Harmony. "How does she rationalize that?"

"The free market has decided that the Vazonian civilization should be ruled by a single, all-powerful corporation for which she is essentially the Chief Executive Officer," said Ulysses. "She does not consider herself to be part of a governing body. All civilians are employees of the parent corporation, and everything is thought of in terms of business. It's a bizarre combination of socialism, capitalism, monarchy, autocracy, anarchy, and maybe even facism if you think about it. But where was I?"

"The Vazakanian constitution," said Peter.

"Right," said Ulysses. "The Vazakanian Constitution gave people the right to sexual freedom, but under the Vazonian Empire, women have once more assumed a secondary role to men. Sexual activity between anything other than a man and a woman that are married to each other is now illegal and punishable by death. Curiously enough, the practice of sex slavery is very common and legal. A woman may enter a marriage with a man as a binding contract for him to provide her with the basic essentials for survival, as long as she'll keep him happy, if you get what I'm saying. And a man may have two wives as long as at least one of them is a sex slave. The ideology of the Vazonian regime is very bizarre. Apparently, this was the way society worked during their civilization's antiquity, which was when this religion was originally practiced. Seems to contradict itself, doesn't it?"

"I guess marriage validates anything a man and a woman do under this religion," said Harmony. "Can men be sex slaves?"

"Absolutely not," said Ulysses. "It says in the Book of Zaxajar, their sacred text, that woman is quote, 'a being given to man by Xiaf to be used as a servant.' Keep in mind that this version of the empire is only thirty years old."

"So they've only been the Vazonian Empire for a very brief part of their history," said Harmony. "This is all very recent."

"Most of the people who once followed the Vazakanian Way are still alive," said Ulysses. "But they've turned their back on their once peaceful lifestyle."

III: Zerpanya walked toward the royal chamber.

She stopped in front of the doors and took a deep breath. The guards let her in. She walked in and knelt before the Queen. The Queen stood and looked down at her.

[Rise,] said the Queen. [I assume that you've located the Shadow Base.]

[No, your highness,] said Zerpanya. She remained on the floor. [We raided one of their outposts and due to my own arrogance, all data files which could have led us to the base were destroyed. But I did encounter someone we'd thought to be dead, someone I'm sure you'd like to hear about.]

[Who?] asked the Queen.

[Your highness, Danya is alive,] said Zerpanya.

[Danya?] asked the Queen. [Which Danya do you speak of?]

[The only Danya I could call by a single name in your presence,] said Zerpanya. [I speak of her.]

[Impossible,] said the Queen. [Surely you're mistaken.]

[Had you been there yourself to see her face,] said Zerpanya. [I know what I saw, your highness. I swear to Xiaf: she lives.]

[How could she have survived?] asked the Queen. [Without being recognized for who she was? How could she have escaped to Troyanya? It's impossible.]

[She was just a girl when she disappeared,] said Zerpanya. [She has grown into an adult.]

[What was the nature of your encounter?] asked the Queen.

[She has joined the resistance,] said Zerpanya [She tricked me and escaped. She's very smart, well-trained, and she's a very formidable opponent.]

[Find her,] said the Queen. [By Xiaf, I must look upon her for myself.]

[We will find her,] said Zerpanya. [I swear to you, I will personally hunt her down.]

[I want her alive,] said the Queen. [Do not fail me again or I will be forced to take something from you. You're very valuable to me. I would hate to have to take too much. If Danya lives, then I must see her.]

[I understand, your highness,] said Zerpanya. [In the meantime, you can read through the profile I've matched this woman to. She has certainly embraced the ways of old. She has turned her back on Xiaf.]

[Find her immediately,] said the Queen. [Before the coming battle. You are aware of our next target, are you not?]

[I am aware,] said Zerpanya. [I will find her before then.]

IV: Jason cried out in agony as the woman slapped him across the face.

"I'm telling you, I don't know anything," said Jason. "I don't know where the fucking base is, and even if I did, I'd die before I'd tell you."

"We know you're lying," said the woman. "You're free to go if you tell us everything. But you won't talk and that's a problem."

"I don't fucking know anything," said Jason. "I got nothing. Torture me all you want. You're wasting your time."

The woman put her finger to her right ear.

"It seems that you might be telling the truth," said the woman. "At least, that's what we think. But there's only one way to know for sure."

The door to the room opened and another woman with a metal case walked in. She put the case down on the table and opened it, taking out a very long needle.

"Hell no," said Jason. "I don't fucking know anything. You're wasting whatever's in that needle."

"We'll see about that," said the other woman.

The other woman took the needle and walked toward Jason.

"This should tell us everything we need to know," she said.

Jason felt the needle plunge into his shoulder. Jason cried out in pain.

The woman with the needle removed it from his shoulder and said something to the uniformed woman. Jason couldn't understand it.

"Where's the base?" she asked.

"I don't know," said Jason. His vision clouded.

V: Danya stepped down onto the solid rock floor of the hangar. An interrogation crew stood waiting. They took the man Danya had never seen before and led him away. A uniformed lieutenant stepped up to the three women.

"Grand General Sazún awaits you in the command center," he said.

"Thank you, lieutenant," said Hatshenya. Danya and Sabenya began following her through the base. They came to the command center. It was a very busy place: full of computer equipment and all sorts of people. There was a man in a white uniform standing up on the command deck studying a large orbital display screen. He looked down at the three women. Danya walked up to him.

"Danya," he said. "It would be nice to see you again were the circumstances not so dire." The two other women stepped up onto the command deck. "General Hatshenya and Commander Sabenya," he said. "I heard your transmission. How did they locate the outpost?"

"A Union soldier we had at the outpost left footprints when he found us," said Danya. "No way we could have known."

"I understand," said the Grand General. "This is most unfortunate."

"What will we do now, Grand General?" asked Hatshenya.

"It is fortunate that you happened to take General Kufán on board that escape shuttle," said the Grand General. "Because he could lead us to our ultimate goal."

"What do you mean, sir?" asked Sabenya. "Who was that man?"

"General Kufán," said the Grand General. "He formerly held my position in the Vazonian Military. But then he attempted to oust Director Zerpanya from her position as the Director of Ven Thar. He failed and was exiled to Troyanya."

"So then he must know many Vazonian secrets," said Sabenya.

"Yes," said the Grand General. "And he has agreed to tell us everything he knows, including the location of San Tun Zaf, which is where all of our imprisoned soldiers are held. General, if you would kindly accompany me to the interrogation room, I would like your opinions as we question him."

VI:

General Hatshenya stood next to Grand General Sazún behind the mirror as the interrogation of the defector took place.

[So how can we be certain that this is the location of San Tun Zaf?] asked the first interrogator.

[Tell us,] said the second. [How can we be sure?]

[The Vazonian military supply chain,] said Kufán. [The logistics of keeping over a thousand people alive in an orbital space station are very hard to cover up. Most shipments of supplies leave from the planet Kovala. The shipments take place over the course of many full days on the planet so as not to draw attention from you. However, this often ties up the spaceports and causes civilian traffic to be delayed.]

"He's right," said Sazún. "Delays at the Kovala spaceport due to military traffic are cyclical."

"This is exactly what we need," said General Hatshenya. She picked up the microphone and spoke to the interrogators. "How can we get into San Tun Zaf unnoticed?" she asked.

The interrogators relayed the question to the defector. He paused. [The spacecraft overhaul schedule,] he said. [As I'm sure you know, Vazonian space stations across the Vazonian Empire regularly host overhaul procedures for the smaller spacecraft in the military fleet. There is often much confusion and misidentification of vessels and I could easily imagine someone getting into San Tun Zaf without being noticed. Getting out will be the problem. They change the codes on the locks every few simulated days. I do not know the master clearance codes that override security. Only four people in the empire do: the Queen, Director Zerpanya of Ven Thar, Supreme Commander Katán who commands all military operations, and General Yaden, the Queen's chief political advisor.]

Hatshenya turned to Sazún. "Do you think he's telling the truth?" she asked. "There are master clearance codes that no one else knows?"

Sazún held the microphone to his mouth. "We want to know more about this master clearance code," he said. "Can it override anything else other than codes at San Tun Zaf?"

The interrogators asked the question.

[That's classified information that even I never had access to,] said General Kufán. [The code is a legend among the ranks of Ven Thar operatives. We all know it exists, but they also say that there are two other master codes and that one must know all three, as well as which of the three can be used to access whichever computer you wish to access.]

"I wouldn't doubt that," said Sazún. "That sounds like Vazonian Command to me."

"Imagine if we could have those codes," said Hatshenya. "How much easier life would be for us."

"Let us not get lost in our dreams," said Sazún. "All we need now is for him to give us an accurate schematic of San Tun Zaf and we can begin planning our liberation of the facility."

Grand General Sazún held the microphone to his mouth and told the interrogators to provide Kufán with some paper and a writing implement. The interrogators did that.

[We would like you to do your best to draw a schematic of San Tun Zaf,] said the first interrogator. [Map out all the points where one can access the central computer of the facility.]

Kufán went to work. Hatshenya watched as he worked.

VII:

Faustemi knelt before the Queen. [Your highness,] he said. [In order to achieve what you ask of me, I must ask your permission to access the forbidden library.]

[The forbidden library,] said the Queen. [What exists within its walls that could possibly assist you in your research?]

[This task takes me into a field of study now banned by Vazonian law,] said Faustemi. [I can grant you immortality, but you must allow me to study the forbidden science.]

The Queen was silent for a moment. [Do it,] she said. [I grant you full access to the forbidden library. May Xiaf bless you in your research.]

[Thank you, your highness,] said Faustemi. [I will begin the research immediately.]

VIII: Director General Ulysses cycled to the next slide.

"Kya zezesha jyanto," said everyone.

"Meaning?" asked General Ulysses.

"Don't go there," said Harmony. "It's an imperative, a command."

"Very good." Said Ulysses. "How do you know it's a command?"

"Ends in zesha," said Harmony. "That's the second person imperative ending for verbs."

"We're picking this up fast," said General Ulysses. "We're making good progress."

IX: General Hatshenya sat near the head of the conference table by Grand General Sazún as she addressed the commanders.

"The operation will be called Operation Host," she said. "Our main objective will be to liberate the prisoners being held in the San Tun Zaf orbital space station. We've obtained the coordinates for the facility. It's located in a small star system called Elpisarn. Our plan of attack will be to first send in a small commando task force to work from within the facility. Once they've established position inside, the Shadow Fleet will begin a frontal assault on the Vazonian fleet stationed around the facility. This will force the Vazonian fleet to focus its attention away from the facility while the task force goes to work."

"How exactly will we insert this commando task force into San Tun Zaf?" asked one of the commanders. "We can't assume that our soldiers will simply walk in with no resistance. This is the Vazonian Empire's highest-level detainment facility."

"The window of opportunity occurs during an overhaul schedule for military spacecraft," said Hatshenya. "During this time, small spacecraft in the Vazonian fleet report to different locations across the empire for their regular overhaul procedures. We will send our task force in a recently stolen military vessel during the overhaul schedule. The vessel was scheduled to be overhauled at San Tun Zaf and we've now confirmed that the vessel has not been removed from the schedule."

"So once inside, what will this task force do?" asked another of the commanders. "How will they manage to commandeer a station as large as this one?" The commander pointed down at the schematic on the table.

"There is a room with direct access to the central computer of the entire facility," said Hatshenya. "This room does not require security clearance to enter. From this access point, our team will remotely unlock all doors in the facility, giving the prisoners freedom and access to the armory. We have now confirmed that over a hundred prisoners at San Tun Zaf are our own soldiers captured from various operations over the course of the war. We can only hope that the Ven Thar interrogation techniques will not have worn them down into mental instability.

Leading this commando task force will be Commander Danya. Are there any questions?"

"What planet are we on now?" asked Danya. "Just so I know."

"This is Earth, Commander," said Grand General Sazún.

7:

I: Commander Danya stood on the command deck of the spacecraft as it approached the docking bay of the space station.

The communicator chimed as the vessel drew closer.

[Communications officer, put them through,] said Danya. She spoke Vazakanian.

The image of a male communications officer appeared on the communication screen.

[Incoming craft, please identify yourself,] he said.

[Assault ship one four zero six yed,] said Danya. [Reporting for routine overhaul.]

[Negative,] said the officer. [We've received orders that all overhaul procedures are cancelled until further notice.]

Danya paused for a moment.

[We've received no such orders,] she said. [Communications officer, did we receive any orders that spoke of cancellation?]

[No, ma'am,] said the communications officer. [No new transmissions have been received.]

Danya looked back up at the screen. [Was this message relayed to all that were to be receiving overhauls?] she asked.

[No details were disclosed,] said the speaker. [Our orders are simply to turn away any vessel that appears for a scheduled overhaul.]

[Is there any indication as to why all overhaul procedures have been cancelled?] asked Danya.

[We received no reason,] said the speaker. [Simply that all procedures are cancelled until further notice.]

[What would you have us do then?] asked Danya. [Should we return to our post? It seems to me that every time we're scheduled for an overhaul, something like this happens. We just want our repairs and we want to return to our posts.]

[Return to your assignment,] said the speaker. [We've been instructed to issue those orders.]

[May we dock with you to at least recharge our oxygen before we leave?] asked Danya. [We're low at the moment. We suspect that it may be leaking out of a micro-fracture. This was supposed to be repaired during the overhaul.]

There was a pause. [Very well, proceed to the docking bay,] said the speaker. [A maintenance crew will greet you there.]

[Thank you,] said Danya. [Preparing to dock. One four zero six yed out.]

The transmission ended. All was silent as the vessel made its way into the docking bay. The sound of electronic motors could be heard in the cabin. Danya walked down the stairs and exited the command deck followed by the rest of the task force. They waited for the pressure to fully equalize and then the ramp was lowered before them. Danya led the task force down into the docking bay.

From the aft of the vessel, a number of men and women wheeled out boxes.

A uniformed officer approached them, eyeing all of the women that were present suspiciously. [What is this?] he asked.

[Supplies,] said Danya. [From Troyanya.]

Two armed men joined the officer. The officer looked at Danya closely.

[Open that box,] he said. [I want to see what's inside it.]

[Yes sir,] said Danya. She went up to the closest box and removed the lid, reaching down into it and gripping the handle of one of the assault rifles. She took a deep breath and then spun around, opening fire on the officer and the the two guards. They fell to the floor as the sound of the gunfire echoed through the docking bay.

"Everyone, go," yelled Danya. She spoke English.

All of the crewmembers and officers from the craft reached into the boxes and took out their own weapons and equipment. They all began running toward the blast door. An alarm began to sound. Danya ran through the docking bay and to the blast door where members of her crew were already setting up explosives. She counted to three and the charges were detonated, opening up a hole in the door. She led everyone through it, navigating through all the hallways and opening fire on the staff as they confronted her. She continued on and turned a corner, but then she quickly dove back behind it as a heavy gun emplacement opened fire on her.

"They've set up gun emplacements," said Danya. "We need a smokescreen."

One of the crew handed Danya a canister with a pin attached to it. Danya pulled the pin and threw it down the hallway. Smoke immediately began to fill the air.

"Formation one pause four," said Danya. "We need a diversion."

Half of the crew remained at the corner and got into formation while Danya led the other half down a side corridor. After going down another series of hallways, she led everyone up a flight of stairs to a blast door. It had a security keypad. Danya stared down at it for a moment.

"This isn't supposed to be here," she said. "This door shouldn't have a lock."

"It looks like this lock was just installed," said one of the other team members.

Danya lifted her communicator to her mouth.

"All units, status report," she said.

"Host four to host one," said the communicator. "In position around the armory. Waiting for door to open. No hostiles present."

"Host three to host two," said the communicator. "Have secured the docking bay. Ready to leave at your command. No hostiles present."

Danya looked down at the keypad in front of her.

"They knew we were coming," she said. "They figured it out."

II: A formation of small warships cruised through space toward a massive assembly of larger warships in orbit around a heavily cratered moon. Inside the warship at the front of the formation, a young pilot checked her monitors and prepared the vessel for combat.

She removed her headset for a moment to adjust it. She was Sabenya.

"All craft prepare to engage time dilation drives," said her communicator. "On my mark: one, two, three, engage."

The young woman engaged the time dilation drive. After a few moments, the craft trembled and the image of the Vazonian fleet appeared on the monitors.

"All units, stay in formation," said the communicator. "Arm weapons and acquire targets."

"Acquiring," said the copilot. He paused. "We have a lock."

"Steady," said the communicator. "Engage."

The young woman opened fire with the rail guns. The enemy fleet began to break formation.

"Incoming craft from the rear," said the communicator. "They're surrounding us."

"What?" asked the young woman. "Who are they?"

"They appear to be Vazonian reinforcements," said the communicator. "All units, break formation. This isn't going to be easy."

Sabenya began to evade gunfire.

III: Danya pushed the button next to the doorframe and a red light flashed before her. She thought for a moment. Her mind was racing.

"Come on, commander," said one of the team. "We have to get in there. "Just shoot it. Blast the damn thing."

"This door has a concussion sensor," said Danya. "You shoot it and it locks down forever. You need to cut it open.

We don't have the time or the equipment, and we don't want to damage the computer either."

"Well, do something," yelled the team member. "We have to get in there."

"Host three to host one," said the communicator. "Multiple hostiles incoming."

"Host four to host one," said the communicator. "Several hostiles approaching our sector. We need the doors open now."

Danya stared down at the keypad for a moment more and then closed her eyes. She opened them and then punched in a sixteen-digit code. The door slid open.

"Let's go," she said.

"That's our commander," said one of the team. "Let's get going here."

The team went inside the room and the computer technicians went to work.

"How long will it take?" asked Danya.

"Don't worry," said one of the technicians. "I can get in very quickly."

Danya waited and watched as the technician worked on the computer. Danya heard footsteps coming up the stairs. She got down on one knee and began firing as the soldiers appeared. She took them down easily. Several more moments passed. Danya turned back to the technicians.

"Done," said one of them. "Let's go."

"Everyone out," said Danya. "Engage hostiles at will."

She waved her hand and the team began moving. She stayed behind as they all left. She went up to the computer and typed in a name. The screen changed and Danya gave it a glimpse before leaving.

Danya ran down one of the hallways away from the team, turning a corner and taking down an armed guard with her assault rifle as she did so. She continued on and came to a corridor lined with doors. She passed a few but then came to one and kicked it open. Jason was inside lying on the floor.

Danya pulled him up onto his feet.

"Time to go," she said.

Danya led Jason down the hallway toward the docking bay. She ran as fast as she could. They made it to the docking bay. There was a firefight taking place inside.

Danya picked a weapon up off the floor and tossed it to Jason. They began running toward the spacecraft.

IV: Sabenya pitched and rolled her spacecraft as her gunners took down the enemy fighters.

"They're everywhere," said Sabenya. "We're not going to last long out here. Come on, Danya. Get everyone out of there."

The craft shuddered as it took a hit.

"Damage report," said Sabenya.

"Main thruster number one failing," said the copilot.

"Shut down main thruster three," said the young woman. "We'll go at half-power."

"Affirmative," said the copilot.

"All units, report," said the communicator.

The young woman pitched the craft to avoid an oncoming attack. One of the gunners took the enemy fighter down as the members of shadow force one reported.

"Shadow force one reporting," said the young woman. "Six damaged but active, two unresponsive, and zero undamaged."

"Shadow force two reporting," said the communicator. "Four damaged but active, four unresponsive, and zero undamaged."

The young woman listened to the communicator. The story was much the same everywhere.

"Let's go," she yelled. "We can't fail."

V: Danya fired her weapon as she made her way toward the spacecraft. She had Jason at her back firing in the other direction.

The two of them made it to the spacecraft and backed their way in.

"Commander," said one of the soldiers. "We weren't going to leave without you."

"Status report," said Danya. "Prisoners."

"One hundred and twenty accounted for," said the soldier. "Eight dead, six wounded. Commandos: forty accounted for, thirteen dead, nine wounded. Preparing for evacuation now."

"Proceed," said Danya. "Input remote codes."

"Yes ma'am," said the soldier. "Vacuum forming. Preparing to open doors."

A moment passed by as the doors opened.

"Over and out," said Danya. She walked upstairs to the command deck. "Communications officer, we're leaving."

VI: "All units, form a perimeter around the entrance to the space station," said the communicator. "The package is leaving the host."

"Shadow force one, follow me," said Sabenya. "We're not out of this yet."

The shadow fleet began to defend the entrance to the space station as the transport vessel left.

"I've never been so happy to see a Vazonian personnel transport in my life," said Sabenya.

"All units, set course for the rendezvous point," said the communicator.

"Setting course now," said the copilot. "All systems clear."

"Engage time dilation drives on my mark," said the communicator. "Three, two, one, engage."

Sabenya engaged the time dilation drive and the craft lurched forward. A short time passed and the craft trembled. The image of the Shadow Fleet appeared on the monitors.

The communicator erupted with cheers.

"This is where we part ways," said the speaker. "Let us all be thankful for the success of this mission."

"Shadow force one, proceed to Shadow Base," said Sabenya. "Mission success."

VII: Zerpanya quietly watched as the Shadow Fleet escaped and then got a lock on their trajectory. They were headed toward the planet Earth. She input the destination to the navigation computer and activated the time dilation drive.

VIII: Jason climbed down out of the transport and waited for Danya. The hangar was full of people that had already exited. A moment passed by and Danya

appeared at the top of the ramp. She walked down to the floor.

"There you are, Commander," said Hatshenya. "Excellent work. This was a vital operation."

"Thank you, ma'am," said Danya.

The roar of spacecraft filled the hangar. A formation of six more craft touched down. From the head of the formation, a crew jumped down to the ground. A young woman took her helmet off. It was Sabenya.

"What the hell took you so long?" she asked. "You almost had everyone killed."

"The door had a keypad lock," said Danya. "With a concussion sensor. Wasn't supposed to be there."

"How did you get it open then?" asked Sabenya

"Guessed the right code," said Danya.

Sabenya laughed. "Only you would do that," she said. "The Queen's not going to be happy about that."

"It only took you two tries," said a man in body armor. "Wish I had that kind of luck. Glad we have you on our side."

IX:

Faustemi cycled through the pages of the book on the projector, seeing a diagram of stem cells on one page and a diagram of a large glass chamber on the other side.

Konsel stepped up to Fuastemi. [What perverted science is this?] he asked.

[The study of genetics,] said Faustemi. [The forbidden science.]

[The Queen allowed you to research genetics?] asked Konsel.

[It is the only way to achieve her goal,] said Konsel. [She seeks immortality. I can give it to her using this science.]

[How?] asked Konsel. [How could anything possibly give the gift of immortality?]

[It can be done,] said Faustemi. [I simply must design a replication machine.]

[A replication machine?] asked Konsel. [What will this replication machine do?]

[It will give the Queen that which she desires,] said Faustemi. [She will live forever.]

[How will she live forever?] asked Konsel. [What will this machine do?]

[The technology is with us,] said Faustemi. [We can make her immortal.]

8:

I: Jason sat at the table with a cut of roast and a baked potato in front of him. He took a bite of the roast and then took a sip of water.

"Good stuff," he said. "You live like kings here compared to that outpost on Troyanya. Haven't had a roast this good in a long time."

A uniformed man that Jason hadn't seen before walked up to the table. He looked at Danya.

"Great work, Commander," he said. "I'm very proud of you." The man looked at Jason for a moment. "Who is this?" he asked.

Jason stood up and shook the man's hand. "Lance Corporal Jason Constantine," said Jason. "I'm a downed American pilot for the Interstellar Union."

"Grand General Sazún," said the man. "I command the resistance."

"Nice to meet you sir," said Jason. "Your people have treated me very well. I must say though, that my people have no idea your resistance exists. Would you let me tell them about it?"

"This is partially why I've come here to you," said Sazún. "I've come here to ask if you will do everything you can to forge an alliance between our resistance and the Interstellar Union. If we could work together, then the Queen's worst nightmare would have come true. That's what we want."

"Makes complete sense," said Jason.

"Do you know if they would be open to the idea?" asked Sazún.

"I'm just a soldier, sir," said Jason. "I do what I'm told to do and I do it well. That's my job."

"I hope they recognize the benefits of working together with us," said Sazún. "We know things about the Vazonian Empire that they do not. We will gladly share our information if they're willing to trust us. We share a common goal: to overthrow the Vazonian regime and to liberate all of the worlds it controls. We want freedom and they want freedom."

"Tell them," said Hatshenya. "Tell your people that we have been fighting the Vazonian regime longer than they have. We originally formed as an underground network of Vazakanian citizens to search for the remaining one. We've always been loyal to the original royal family."

"What's the remaining one?" asked Jason.

"A symbol that gives us all hope," said Sazún. "We hope that someday, a surviving member of the royal family will lead us to victory against the Queen. It's just a myth however. We've learned that we must lead ourselves."

"Just curious, sir: when will I return to my people?" asked Jason. "So I can deliver your message?"

"That's the other reason I've come here," said Sazún. "You will leave immediately. Danya will drop you off near the USPDF base."

"Sounds like a plan," said Jason. "Thank you all for keeping me safe."

II: Jason followed Danya down the hallway. She stopped at her room, entering it. Jason followed behind her, closing the door behind them as she unziupped her flight suit.

"So this is goodbye, huh?" he asked. "I might never see you again."

"You'll always have to say goodbye to everyone you meet in life," said Danya. "You can't avoid that."

Jason paused. "So, what you're saying," he said. "Is that with everyone you ever meet in life, you'll always never see them again at some point?"

Danya was silent.

"And, under that logic, it's not even worth getting to know people then," said Jason. "Right? That sums up who you are pretty well, doesn't it?" He shook his head. "So how do you expect to win the war if you're going to think like that?"

"Just being realistic," said Danya. "Every beginning has an end."

"I have another question for you then," said Jason. "Do you ever smile? Have you ever smiled? Do you know how to smile?"

"There will be plenty of time for smiling after we win the war," said Danya.

"But what if we don't win?" asked Jason. "What if it never happens in your lifetime? Do you want to die knowing you've never once enjoyed yourself? If you like to be so realistic, then you obviously know that you could die on any given day in the resistance. So, knowing that, how can you go through life without ever laughing or smiling or even making an effort to have fun? What's holding you back from doing that? What are you afraid of?"

Danya was silent. She stepped out of the flight suit. Her traditional libranya lay beneath it.

"Let's go," she said.

"You're not even going to answer?" asked Jason. "You're just going to ignore the question?"

"You don't hear me dissecting your personality," said Danya.

"I'd fucking love to hear you tell me what you think of me," said Jason. "Because that would show me you can feel emotion. That would show me you're capable of dreaming for a better future."

Danya was silent. She opened the door and began walking through the base. Jason followed her.

"You're unbelievable," he said. "I sure hope you'll understand what I'm talking about someday."

III: Zerpanya hacked her way through the terrain with a large knife. She knew the base was close.

An air transport roared overhead. Zerpanya ran back to her spacecraft and fired it up. She lifted it off the ground and began her pursuit.

She urged the craft forward and began following the other vessel. It suddenly changed its course and began heading east.

The other vessel charged over the Pacific Ocean and headed toward the western United States where it was nighttime. The vessel abruptly charged downward. Zerpanya watched it all the way.

IV: Danya pulled her helmet off and looked back at Jason.

"Is it gone?" she asked.

"I'm not picking it up on our radar," said Jason. He paused. "So where are we going now?"

"Los Angeles," said Danya. "It's a big city. We can easily disappear for a little while before we bring you to the base."

"So where are we going land then?" asked Jason. "Did you stop to think about that? This is a spacecraft. These things don't exist on this planet except in the military."

"Airport," said Danya. "We'll just pose as a private jet. It's nighttime. No one will know anything unless they get too close. But we won't let them get too close."

"Whatever you say," said Jason.

Danya put her helmet back on and changed the frequency of her communicator. She started hailing the airport. She made it sound as convincing as she could.

"Ma'am, are you threatening me?" asked the communicator.

"No, I'm not threatening you," said Danya. "I'm up here in a jet and I want to get down there on Earth. Obviously, a mistake was made. Do you have any available hangars? That's all we're asking for."

"Alright, you have permission to land," said the communicator. "You're lucky I'm the one in the tower and not someone else. This is an international airport. We have a tight schedule and, next time, you need to make sure we're expecting you."

"Thank you very much," said Danya.

Danya piloted the spacecraft down to the airport and did her best imitation of a jet plane, cruising down the runway and coming to a stop near the end.

"Could you open the door and ask them which hangar is ours?" asked Danya.

She watched as Jason did just that. He talked to the crew for a moment and then returned.

"I told them that this was an experimental model of air transport that I invented myself," he said. "I told them that I believed it was the future of transportation and then I asked them which hangar was ours. They pointed to that one over there."

"Thank you," said Danya. She guided the spacecraft into the hangar.

She and Jason exited the vessel and met up with the crew that was looking on.

"Remember this day," said Jason. "You saw the first hypercraft ever created."

V: Director General Ulysses nodded his head as the last group finished their scene.

"Very good," said Ulysses. "We'll all have to work on our accents and the more advanced aspects of the language, but as it stands, we can all now speak the Vazonian Language. Ladies and gentlemen, we're ready to take on the Vazonian Empire."

There was a knock on the door. "Come in," said Ulysses.

The door opened and a man in a suit entered. "Sir, we've detected unusual activity at the LAX airport.

Witnesses report seeing spacecraft landing there. The air traffic control tower reports several unscheduled landings."

"Excellent," said Ulysses. "Our first challenge. Harmony and Peter, I want you to look into this."

"Yes, sir," said Harmony.

VI: Danya opened the doors to the spaceport and Jason followed her inside. They made it to their hangar and went into it. Danya began retracting the doors and, as Jason watched her, he felt something press against his skull.

"Don't move," said a female voice. "Don't say a word."

He felt an arm wrap around him and pull him into the shadows.

"Could you warm up the spacecraft?" asked Danya.

"Don't answer," said the voice. Jason was silent.

"Jason?" asked Danya. She looked around. She stepped into the light. "Come and get me, Director," she said. "It's me you want. What is he worth to you? I know you're here. Come and get me."

Jason felt himself being pushed out into the open with the gun against his head.

"Hello, Danya," said Zerpanya. "You have a date with the Queen."

"You think so?" asked Danya. "Tell me: what happened to your eye? Did the Queen take it because you failed her?"

"No, my dear," said Zerpanya. "A man I once loved took this eye from me. And he paid the price for it. He's about to pay the price for it again. I'm going to take you straight to the Queen before the coming battle of the Solar System. The timing will be perfect."

"What are you talking about?" asked Danya. "What battle of the Solar System?"

"Don't you know?" asked Zerpanya. "Surely the resistance has the intelligence. At this very moment, the Vazonian fleet is on its way here. They should be arriving at any moment. And once they do, they will take the system, ensuring the victory of the Vazonian Empire in name of Xiaf. Luckily, you happened to stop by just in time. Cooperate now. I have snipers on both of you. Drop your weapon. It will make this a whole lot easier."

Danya dropped her pistol and walked up to Zerpanya.

"Take that gun off of his head," said Danya. "What is he worth to you? Why would you even touch a man with no faith in Xiaf?"

Zerpanya was silent. She held the gun up.

"It's a stunner," she said. "It's non-lethal. You should ask yourself the same thing about faith in Xiaf. I remember a time when you also believed in Xiaf."

Jason made his move. He threw Zerpanya to the ground. Danya began wrestling with her, but the woman managed to throw Danya down on her face.

"Run," yelled Danya. "Warn the others."

[Snipers,] said Zerpanya. [Fire.]

Jason picked up Danya's pistol and charged into the spacecraft. Tranquilizer darts impacted on the side of the vessel as he closed the door and powered it up, pushing it as hard as he could. He trembled as he set a course for the last destination the craft had come from.

VII: General Hatshenya stood in front of the map next to Grand General Sazún.

"So you think the fleet will be safer here?" asked Hatshenya.

"Much safer," said Sazún. "This system is far more remote than any we've ever stationed the fleet at, and it also gives us a quick route to Earth."

An officer walked up to them.

"Sir, the American pilot needs to speak with you immediately."

"They've returned?" asked Hatshenya. "Tell them we're in a meeting and we'll be out shortly."

"It's only the American pilot," said the officer. "Commander Danya did not return with him."

Hatshenya and Sazún looked at each other.

"Send him in immediately," said Hatshenya.

"Yes, ma'am," said the officer.

He disappeared and Jason ran up the stairs.

"An invasion is coming to Earth," he said. "They'll arrive anytime now. Danya told me to warn you."

"How do you know this?" asked Sazún.

"They captured Danya," said Jason. "We tried to lose them in Los Angeles, but they found us and captured her. I escaped. She told me to warn you."

"Our greatest fear has come to pass then," said Sazún. "So now we must prepare to fight: prepare to give aid to the Interstellar Union. Call an emergency conference. We must collect ourselves."

VIII: Danya calmly walked with the agents and Zerpanya toward the royal chamber of the palace.

Zerpanya walked up to the messenger at the door. The messenger entered the royal camber and quickly returned, opening the door for the group. Danya went into the chamber. The two agents and Zerpanya knelt, but Danya stood.

Danya stared coldly at the Queen. The Queen walked up to Danya, saying nothing. Tears came to the Queen's eyes.

[I tried to prepare myself for this,] said the Queen. She wiped her tears away. [I did everything I could so there would be no tears.] She stared at Danya for a moment. [But to see you here now: all grown up after you've been gone for all these years.] The Queen shook her head. [And you're beautiful, such a beautiful young woman. I knew you would be. Look what you've grown up to be.] The Queen looked at the others in the room. [Zerpanya, good work. You three can leave.]

[But your highness, who will protect you?] asked Zerpanya.

[Protect me from what?] asked the Queen.

[This traitor filth,] said Zerpanya. [This woman is a traitor to the Vazonian Empire. She's trained to kill you.]

[She won't kill me,] said the Queen. [In her heart, she loves me. Go on: get out of here. I need to be alone with my daughter.]

The agents and Zerpanya all looked at each other. [Go,] yelled the Queen.

Zerpanya and the agents hurried out of the royal chamber. Danya watched them go and then turned to the Queen. The Queen fingered the fabric of Danya's traditional Vazakanian outfit.

[What are you wearing?] asked the Queen. [Even under the Vazakanian tradition, black is not fit for a royal princess. Black is the dress of a commoner.]

"Well, your highness," said Danya. She spoke English. "I'm not a princess anymore."

[What language do you speak now?] asked the Queen. [This is not our language. You're a princess of the Vazonian Empire. Honor your heritage by speaking your language.]

"No," said Danya. "I speak the language of a people that are free. Vazonian freedom is a lie. Your obsession with this ancient religion is sickening and a disease on the Vazakanian civilization. You know in your heart that it's all a lie you used to gain power. And yet you sleep soundly at night."

"You don't know what you say," said the Queen. She spoke English. "The good I have done for our civilization can only be compared to what Queen Vazakanya herself did for our civilization. I salvaged it while it was on the edge of collapse and I turned it into greatness."

"Listen to you," said Danya. "You mention your own name in the same breath as our Great Queen Vazakanya. Think before you speak. What are you: a poser, a usurper, a traitor. You're obsessed with a religion you know to be a lie. Why do you continue to put on this act? You say you're a woman of Xiaf as you murder people needlessly in the name of faith. Tell me: what is faith? What is it to you, if not an excuse to kill and sieze power?"

"To have faith in Xiaf is to be pure," said the Queen. "We must all do as Xiaf asks us. Xiaf asks of me to sacrifice."

"It's a lie," said Danya. "You've created an empire that now controls well over half of a galaxy and the most diverse population a single ruler has ever ruled. And you think you can simply convince everyone under your rule to believe in this ancient religion. They do not. They pretend to and live in fear of you."

"If you knew what I knew, my darling, then you would realize the lies you've been told," said the Queen. "It's poisoned your mind. Everything you think you know is a lie, Danya. In time, you'll come to realize that."

"And what, might I ask, do you know that I don't?" asked Danya. "Tell me, your highness. Enlighten me."

"Don't call me your highness," said the Queen. "Don't be so absurd."

"Then what do you suppose I should call you?" asked Danya.

"I'm your mother," said the Queen. "I raised you myself and loved you. You cannot escape that past as much as you wish you could. For thirteen years of your life, you loved me and called me your mother. You looked up to me, you spent precious moments of joy and happiness with me, and here you stand now as if you don't remember any of it. I'm your mother and I will always be your mother."

"You are not my mother now," said Danya. "Listen to you: you're insane. You're obsessed with a lie. You kill people and rationalize it with that lie. And why did the sight of me bring tears to your eyes if you know I intend to kill you? I can't kill you until I know that."

"Kill me, Danya?" asked the Queen. "After all the love I've given you and after all I did to make you happy? Do you know the pain and the grief I went through when we discovered that note you left, the one that said you had drowned yourself in the sea?"

"I never cared to think about that," said Danya. "I never really considered it to be that important. I was disgusted with you, as I should have been."

"I cried for nine days," said the Queen. "It hit me hard, Danya."

Danya shook her head. "You don't love me," said Danya. "You're incapable of love or compassion. You destroyed the true royal family. You're a murderer."

More tears came to the Queen's eyes.

"Do you even have any remorse for what you did?" asked Danya. "Do you even have the slightest regret for your actions?" Danya shook her head. "No, you don't. You slaughtered every living member of our sacred family, and it's never once crossed your mind that you might be a murderer. Where do you find the will to love me? What motivates that love? What drives it? I will not kill you until I know."

The Queen was now crying harder than Danya had ever seen her cry.

"Why are you crying?" demanded Danya. "Tell me now."

The Queen continued to cry.

"You're pathetic," said Danya. "I'll enjoy killing you."

Danya approached the Queen.

"I have always loved you," said the Queen. "Always. Your words are hurtful."

Danya hesitated but continued walking toward the Queen.

"Always," said the Queen. "You simply don't know who you are, Danya. You're the world to me: more than the empire and more than all space and time."

Danya stopped and looked at the Queen. The Queen wiped her tears away.

"Then tell me," said Danya. "Who am I really?"

"You, Danya, are the remaining one," said the Queen. "You're the child of the royal family that I spared. Your true name is Na Danya Vih Zalenya. I saved you because I looked into your eyes and saw the innocence of a pure spirit. I have always loved you, Danya, always, from the first moment I saw you. I had such compassion for you that I raised you as my own daughter."

Danya was silent. She stepped up closer to the Queen. "Then give me the throne," said Danya. "If what you say is true, then it's my birthright to have it."

The Queen's expression changed.

"There is no sincerity to your words, Danya," said the Queen. "It's your birthright to have it, but you fear the throne." The Queen nodded. "Director Zerpanya has told me all about you: how you hide your past from the resistance, and how you isolate yourself from the others there. You fear your true identity, Danya. You fear your past. You haven't even the strength of will to confess it to those you fight with. A dangerous fighter you are, but on the inside, you lack willpower. You don't want to be Queen, Danya. The throne is only fit for one who wants it. It was the law of the traditions of old: the heir to the throne was he or she who desired it most. So ask yourself: what would you do if I decided to relinquish the throne to you?" The Queen nodded her head. "I can see it in your eyes now: the fear. You're afraid. And you know what I say is true. I invite you to come and be my daughter again. The resistance will soon fall. Be my daughter. I know you still love me, and, perhaps in time, you will not fear the throne."

Danya was silent for a moment. Without a word, she turned and walked out of the royal chamber, passing Zerpanya and Kedán on the way.

Danya walked past them and exited the royal palace.

IX:
The Queen sat on her throne as Zerpanya and the two agents rushed in.

[Oh, your highness, I'm so glad you're safe,] said Kedán.

[Shall I hunt her down and kill her?] asked Zerpanya.

[No,] said the Queen. [She's not a threat to us. She's afraid of what she is and she will be forever.]

[But your highness,] said Kedán. [She wants to overthrow you.]

[Let her want to,] said the Queen. [She'll never be able to. She fears her identity. That's her weakness.]

[Your highness, with all due respect, I don't think you should have just let her go,] said Kedán. [She can still damage our empire.]

[I know that girl,] said the Queen. [That's what she is: she's a girl. No matter how old she grows to be, she will always be a girl.]

[Your highness, that woman is still a traitor,] said Zerpanya. [How could you simply let her walk out of the palace?]

[Because I love her,] said the Queen. [Don't worry about her. She's powerless. We must now concentrate on the invasion of the Solar System.]

9:

I: Jason climbed into the spacecraft and put his helmet on.

"Tell them of our plan and urge them to contact us immediately," said Grand General Sazún. "We will coordinate our defense of this planet when the time comes to do so."

"Yes, sir," said Jason. He closed the cockpit and lifted the craft up off the ground, piloting it across the continental United States toward Washington DC. He looked down over the capital to the familiar shape of the Pentagon. He tuned into the frequency that he'd been instructed to tune into and he spoke.

"Can anyone hear me?" he asked. "Does anyone copy?"

"Who are you?" asked the communicator. "How did you get onto this channel?"

"Lance Corporal Jason Constantine of the United States Planetary Defense Force," said Jason. "I was captured by the Vazonian Empire in battle and I managed to escape back here with the help of a Vazonian resistance group called No Kasanosi. They wish to deliver a message to the Interstellar Union."

II: Ulysses' compad chimed. He answered it.
"Director General Ulysses," he said.

"Sir, there's an unidentified spacecraft outside that's contacted us," said Harmony. "The description fits the images of the spacecraft seen at LAX. The pilot calls himself Lance Corporal Jason Constantine, saying that he escaped from the Vazonian Empire with the help of a resistance group."

"I'll be there immediately," said General Ulysses. He leapt to his feet and hurried into the command center. He stepped up to the communicator. "This is Director General Henry Ulysses, Director of the Central Intelligence Agency and General of the United States Planetary Defense Force. To whom do I speak?"

"My name is Lance Corporal Jason Constantine," said the pilot. "I was shot down over Troyanya on mission to destroy a piracy base. A resistance group called No Kasanosi took me in and helped me escape back here to Earth. I have a message to deliver from them."

"Constantine?" asked Ulysses. "This is General Ulysses. What's your best time running a mile?"

"Four fifty three, sir," said Constantine. "I did it at twenty-nine palms."

"Is there a resistance, soldier?" asked General Ulysses. "Is that how you say you escaped?"

"Yes, sir," said Constantine. "And they have an urgent message for us. I'd like to speak with you immediately."

"We're sending someone out to escort you inside," said General Ulysses. He turned away from the microphone. "Let's go people. This could be our big break. Bring this soldier to the conference room." He turned back to the microphone. "Land your spacecraft, soldier. You and I are going to talk all about this resistance."

Ulysses hurried out of the command center to the conference room. After a few moments, two guards walked into the room with the young pilot.

"Sir," said Constantine. "The resistance has been fighting the Vazonian Empire since Jonarka rose to power. They know how the empire fights, they know how the empire thinks, and they share our goal of wanting to overthrow the Queen and liberate all the systems she controls. They would like to form an alliance with the Interstellar Union. They say that an alliance between us and them would be the Queen's worst nightmare. But the urgent message is that an invasion of Earth is imminent. And they would like to assist us in our defense of our planet."

Ulysses stared at Constantine.

"You've done your planet and your country proud, soldier," said General Ulysses. "How do we get in touch with this resistance? Where are they located?"

"They're based right here on Earth," said Constantine. "In the Himalayan Mountain Range. They would like to coordinate the defense of this star system with us because they know exactly how the empire will attack."

"Then that's what we're going to do, soldier," said General Ulysses. "I've never been more proud of any soldier in my entire life. Let's beat these sons of bitches back to the edge of the galaxy."

"Let me go up there and fight," said Constantine. "I'm not going to sit and watch the battle I've trained for my whole life."

"Soldier," said General Ulysses. "You've done your part in the war. You've performed bravely and you've made yourself a hero. If I had my way, you'd be going right back up there to fight, but it couldn't possibly happen. You need to be debriefed, your health needs to be tested: it's far too much of a risk to send you back up there."

"That's bullshit, sir," said Constantine. "With all due respect. If you don't want me to fight, then you're going to have to stop me first."

Constantine walked away. General Ulysses followed after him. "You're making a mistake, soldier," said General Ulysses. "I know how you feel right now. I've been there before. It's not worth it."

"I'll be the judge of that," said Constantine. "Sir, if I don't go up there after all I've done, then I will not be able to live with myself. Whether we win or lose this battle, everything I've done for this country, for this world, and for the Interstellar Union will be meaningless to me if I can't go up and defend the one place I swore I'd die for. If that makes me a criminal, sir, then so be it. I will be a criminal."

Two security guards rushed up to General Ulysses. He put his arms out and stopped them from pursuing after Constantine.

"Let him go," said General Ulysses. "If he wants to uphold the oath he took when he entered the armed forces, then who am I to stop him?"

III:
Danya piloted the stolen spacecraft off the ground and up through the atmosphere. She set Earth as her destination and hit select. The craft began charging through space. And once the time dilation drive disengaged, Danya found herself behind a massive fleet of Vazonian warships.

She picked up the communicator and tuned it to the frequency of the No Kasanosi headquarters.

"No Kasanosi," she said. "No Kasanosi, do you read me? This is Danya."

"Danya?" asked the communicator. "You're alive?"

"I'll be there as fast as I can," said Danya.

Danya pushed forward on the throttle and began charging through the Vazonian fleet. She'd never seen anything like it before. The fleet was massive.

An alarm sounded. Shots were being fired at her. Danya pulled back on the steering and sent the craft into a loop. The Vazonian fighter was now in front of her. But the spacecraft she was in had no weapons or armor.

The fighter pulled up and did a loop of its own so that it was now behind Danya again. She piloted her spacecraft into a series of dives and flips and the fighter matched each one of them. Her spacecraft wasn't maneuverable enough. Off in the distance, Danya spotted a Vazonian carrier. Danya began charging toward it, continuing to dive and pull up and move sideways as she did so, not allowing the fighter a clean shot. Danya made it right to the side of the Vazonian carrier, and then she pulled up on the steering, sending her flying over the carrier as the fighter crashed into it.

"Shadow base to Danya, did you just take that carrier out?" asked the communicator.

"Consider it a gift," said Danya.

"Good job, Danya," said the speaker. "Now hurry. We need you to do more things like that."

"Yes, sir," said Danya.

She piloted her spacecraft down through the atmosphere and to the Shadow Base. She waited for the cabin pressure to equalize and then she exited the craft. Jason and General Hatshenya were there to greet her. Danya looked away from both of them.

"How did you escape the Queen?" asked Hatshenya.

Danya said nothing.

Jason stared at her. "You're hiding something from everyone, aren't you?" he asked. "And you always have been."

Danya began walking through the base. Hatshenya and Jason followed her to the command center. Sazún was up on the command deck in front of the battle projector. Danya went up to him.

"Commander," he said. "Jason here managed to convince the Solarian fleet to coordinate their operations with us. As the ranking field commander of the fleet, you're the only one I trust to lead this attack in space. I'm going to put you into an assault ship."

"Yes sir," said Danya.

"I want to go with you," said Jason. "I'm here to fight."

"Then let's get going," said Danya.

Danya led Jason through the complex to the hangar. There was a Vazakanian assault ship waiting there.

"Suit up," said Danya.

"I believe this is yours," said Jason. He gave Danya her pistol. "I picked it up off the floor of the hangar."

Danya took the pistol and holstered it. They both suited up. Danya climbed into the assault ship and helped

Jason strap into the turret position. She showed him how to operate the weapon. Danya then strapped herself into the cockpit next to the co-pilot, and after everything had been prepared, she piloted the craft out of the hangar and up through the atmosphere. As the assault ship approached the battle, Danya could make out the shapes of all the warships and Solarian defense platforms.

"Shadow Fleet," said Danya. "Shadow One. All shadow leaders, do you read me?"

Her headset erupted into a chorus of confirmations.

"United Nations fleet," she said. "You read me? Shadow One of No Kasanosi here."

"Shadow One, this is Alpha Leader of the USPDF," said the speaker. "We read you loud and clear." There was a pause. "Shadow One, we're going to have to get right up in their faces and hit 'em hard."

"Shadow Base to Shadow One," said Sazún. "I want you lead our own fleet in breaking through to the other side of the Vazonian fleet so we can surround them."

"Try and break through the Vazonian fleet?" asked Danya. "That'll be very dangerous."

"But if it works, we'll have a very good chance of success," said Sazún. "Send the cruisers in first, along with the assault ships. We have enough cruisers to put up a real fight and the assault ships can defend them from enemy fighters. Keep our destroyers and our carriers back."

"Yes sir," said Danya. "Alpha leader, Shadow One. We're going to break through the enemy fleet to surround them. Stay here while we hit them from the rear."

"Shadow One, we copy," said the speaker. "Alpha leader to alpha force, all PDP's get ready."

"Shadow One to Shadow Fleet," said Danya. "Cruisers regroup. Target enemy carriers. Assault ships, regroup and defend cruisers. Destroyers and carriers, stay back and only engage if necessary."

"Shadow Three to Shadow One," said the speaker. "We copy. All cruisers, follow my lead."

The rest of the shadow units confirmed the orders as well.

Danya pushed the throttle forward. "Be alert," she said. "Here we go."

The assault ship charged toward the enemy fleet. Danya brought the craft to the front of the formation. She looked at her radar.

"Fighters approaching," she said. "Gunners, engage."

Danya sent the ship charging through the cloud of fighters as the roar of the rail guns began filling the craft. Danya could see the enemy fighters being ripped apart all around her. She maneuvered to avoid the debris as she neared the Vazonian carriers.

"Fire missiles," said Danya. "On my command."

"I need you to get me closer," said the co-pilot. "We're out of range."

Danya pushed the throttle forward and the craft began charging straight toward the lead carrier.

The copilot looked through the targeting screen. "A little closer," he said. "Just a little closer."

The carrier began firing its guns at the assault ship. Danya had to maneuver to avoid it. She pitched and rolled the craft.

"Got it," said the co-pilot. "I have a lock."

"Fire," said Danya.

"One, two, three missiles away," said the co-pilot.

Danya pulled up on the steering and sent the craft sharply back in the opposite direction as the missiles impacted on the carrier. She checked the rear monitor and watched as one of the missiles impacted on the carrier's starboard thruster, blowing it out and sending the carrier spinning. The carrier crashed into an enemy cruiser, ripping it in half.

"Good work," said Danya. She checked the screen in front of her. "More fighters incoming. Gunners, engage."

The sound gunfire again filled the craft.

Danya piloted the craft around, maneuvering it to avoid enemy fire and giving the gunners room to shoot down fighters. As the time passed by, Danya looked out over the battle and didn't like what she saw.

"Shadow Base to Shadow One," said Sazún. "We're losing too many cruisers. The enemy has sent in their destroyers and they're tearing our cruisers apart. Send in our destroyers. Tell them to keep the enemy destroyers away from our cruisers."

"Yes sir," said Danya. "Shadow One to Shadow Four. You copy?"

"Shadow Four to Shadow One, we hear you loud and clear," said the speaker. "What do you want us to do?"

"Shadow Four, defend cruisers," said Danya. "Protect them."

"Shadow One, we copy," said the speaker. "All destroyers, target enemy destroyers and keep them away from our cruisers."

"Shadow Base to Shadow Four," said Sazún. "Hurry. Those destroyers are ripping us up."

Danya piloted the craft toward an enemy destroyer. "Gunners, target that destroyer," she said.

The sound of gunfire filled the craft. The destroyer didn't fire back at her. It had all of its guns focused on a Vazakanian cruiser.

"Co-pilot," said Danya. "Fire missiles."

"Missiles away," said the co-pilot.

Danya watched as the missiles impacted on the destroyer, knocking a large hole in it. Danya could see various objects being sucked out of the destroyer through the hole and into space. But the Destroyer continued firing at the cruiser. The cruiser was in bad shape. Danya watched as the enemy destroyer began charging at the cruiser.

"It's a suicide mission," said Jason.

The destroyer crashed into the cruiser. Danya looked out across the battle. The scene wasn't much different wherever she looked.

IV: [Your highness, a messenger has arrived from the battle,] said General Katán.

[Good,] said the Queen. [Put the messenger through.]

The Queen waited a moment.

[Your highness,] said the speaker. [The Union knew we were going to invade. They were waiting for us.]

[Impossible,] said the Queen. [How could they know about the invasion?]

[Well, your highness,] said the speaker. [The resistance is working together with the Union.]

The Queen rose to her feet. [Traitors,] she yelled. [They must be cleansed of their filth. We will crush them. We will destroy them all. There will be no survivors. Hail the resistance. Ask them why they fight in this battle. Offer them Xiaf. Tell them that if they convert, we will spare them and grant them amnesty from their treason. And tell them that this is their final offer. We will no longer take prisoners. All will be killed. And make it seem as if I have made this decision in reaction to their response when asked why they fight.]

V: Jason had the fighter in his sights. He pulled the trigger. The fighter shattered into pieces. He saw another fighter. He rotated the turret and looked through the sights, lining the fighter up with the third hash mark away from the center cross.

Jason pulled the trigger again. It was another hit.

"Shadow one to all units," said Danya. "Vazonian fleet is falling back. They're hailing us."

"What do you mean?" asked Jason.

"Trying to speak to us," said Danya. "Listen."

Jason listened to his headset. "No Kasanosi, No Kasanosi," it said. "Nay bemi nu dranán vih Xiaf."

"Shadow One to Shadow Base," said Danya. "You hear this? Vazonian fleet wants to talk."

"Cease fire and answer it," said Sazún. "We'll see what they have to say, but do not stray too far away from them."

"Shadow One to alpha leader," said Danya. "You read us?"

"Alpha leader to Shadow One," said the speaker. "We read you loud and clear. Do you know what happened?"

"Enemy fleet has ceased fire and has hailed us," said Danya. "Maneuver into position around them. Surround them. I'll do the talking."

"Yes, ma'am," said the speaker. "Go ahead." There was a pause. "Alpha leader to Alpha fleet, follow the Shadow fleet. Let's listen in."

"Vazonian fleet, this is Shadow One," said Danya. "What do you want from us?"

"The Great Queen wishes to make you an offer," said the Speaker. "What is your cause in this battle?"

"Simple," said Danya. "We fight for freedom, freedom from the oppression of the Queen."

"But are you not yourselves Vazonians?" asked the speaker. "Are you not all children of your Lord Xiaf?"

"No," said Danya. "The Vazonian identity is a lie. We're just people that don't like being told how to think and live. We believe in having the freedom to do what we want and having the freedom of will to make our own decisions. We don't need Xiaf to tell us what to do. We're strong enough to think and feel on our own."

There was a long pause.

"Who are you?" asked the speaker. "What is your name?"

"I'm Shadow One," said Danya. "I speak for the resistance. Together, we plan on overthrowing the Queen and restoring freedom to the galaxy. And you will never stop us."

There was another pause. "We will relay this answer to the Great Queen," said the speaker.

Jason watched the Vazonian fleet through the monitor of his turret. He picked out a target.

VI: Danya waited for the response from the Queen. The Vazonian fleet was now in a very tight formation and the U.N. fleet and Vazakanian fleets now had it completely surrounded.

"Vazonian fleet to Shadow One," said the speaker. "Do you copy?"

"Shadow One to Vazonian Fleet," said Danya. "Have you made a decision?"

"The Great Queen has offered amnesty for all members of the resistance on one condition," said the speaker.

"Name it," said Danya.

"You must convert to the faith of Xiaf," said the speaker. "You must give up your ways of filth and perversion."

"And what reason would we have to do that?" asked Danya. "Why should I or the people of the galaxy do any such thing?"

"The Great Queen gave no reason or explanation," said the speaker. "That was all she said. She offers you a chance to become a faithful servant of Xiaf and to wash your hands of the blood you've spilled. You must covert to our faith and give up your filth."

"And the planet Earth?" asked Danya. "What about Earth?"

"The Great Queen has ordered that we are to continue with the invasion, but we will spare you and your resistance if you agree," said the speaker. "The Great Queen says that this is your last offer of peace. No longer will we take prisoners. You betray the empire, then you will die."

"We will not waste our time negotiating with you," said Danya. "Shadow One, out."

There was no response. "Shadow fleet, attack," said Danya. "For Earth."

Danya pushed the throttle forward and began charging toward the enemy fleet.

"All warships follow me and wait for my command," she said.

Danya looked around to her right and left. The entire Shadow Fleet and the Solarian fleet were right with her. She led the fleet closer and closer until she could see the enemy guns with her own eyes and then she spoke into the communicator.

"Shadow One to Shadow fleet," she said. "Fire."

She ordered the Solarian fleet to fire as well. She then watched as the enemy warships were riddled with gunfire. There was no room for them to run.

"Shadow One to Shadow fleet," said Danya. "Fire missiles."

She gave the same order to the Solarian fleet. Her own co-pilot launched five missiles as both the Shadow and Solarian fleets all bombarded the enemy fleet with missiles at the same time. The enemy began firing back and broke its formation. They began spreading out to avoid the barrage.

"Shadow One to Shadow Two," said Danya. "Launch fighters and bombers. Bombers go after the carriers and cruisers, fighters go after the destroyers, assault ships, and other fighters."

"Shadow Two to Shadow One," said the speaker. "We copy. Launching fighters and bombers now."

Danya began guiding the assault ship around through the battle, evading enemy fire and putting the craft in position for the gunners to take down the enemy targets.

She looked in her rear monitor. A diamond formation of Vazonian fighters was behind her.

"Turret, break them up," said Danya.

Danya watched the monitor as the formation of fighters broke apart. She hit the forward thrusters to slow the assault ship down. One of the fighters charged past the assault ship above it.

"The fighter that just passed us," said Danya. "That's our target."

She began pursuing it as the forward gunner began trying to shoot it down. But then an alarm sounded through the craft.

"We've been hit," said Danya. "Where is it?"

"Got it," said the communicator. "You owe me, Danya."

"Sabenya," said Danya. "Thank you."

"You've got some damage," said Sabenya. "Your top right thruster is out."

"Everyone, watch out," said Danya. "We've been slowed down to half-power. We're an easier target."

"Shadow Base to Shadow One," said the speaker. "This is Sazún. Danya, come back to Earth. You're too important to us. I don't want you fighting in a crippled assault ship."

"Shadow Base, this is Shadow One," said Danya. "I'm not going anywhere. Gunners, we're going to fight on. Stay sharp."

Danya began piloting the craft toward the battle again. It didn't take long. Fighters began to approach the assault ship.

"Here they come," said Danya. "Open fire."

The vibrations from the rail guns echoed through the inside of the cabin.

VII: General Ulysses watched the displays.

"It's working, Henry," said one of the officers in the bunker. "The battle has turned in our favor."

"Thank this Vazakanian resistance group," said General Ulysses. "They're leading the charge for us." General Ulysses turned to Peter. "You were correct, Peter. It appears that many Vazonians have rejected their Queen and have formed an organized and armed resistance."

"They're doing great out there," said the President of the United States. "Look at how they fight."

"Yes, their formations are tight and their tactics are sound," said General Ulysses. "They know what they're doing very well."

VIII:

Jason pulled the trigger, aiming for the port thruster of the enemy carrier. He hit it and it blew out, sending the carrier spinning out of control. Another target caught his eye. He aimed at it and pulled the trigger, destroying it as well. He looked around for another target. He couldn't find any.

"Enemy carrier," said Danya. "Surrender to us, or we will be forced to destroy you."

"For Xiaf and for the Queen," said the speaker.

Jason could make out the shape of a massive carrier as it began charging toward one of the Shadow carriers. He targeted it and began firing. Both the Shadow Fleet and the Solarian fleet opened fire on it. It shattered into pieces.

The communication channel erupted into cheers.

"Mission complete," said Danya.

"Alpha Leader to Shadow One," said the speaker. "You guys saved our asses."

"This is Director General Henry Ulysses of the United States Central Intelligence Agency and United

States Planetary Defense Force," said the communicator. "Whoever you are, Shadow One, the United States is forever grateful for your help."

"Sir, my name is Commander Danya," said Danya. "We look forward to working with you more often."

"We will take your help anytime you can give it to us," said General Ulysses. "You've earned our trust."

"Shadow Base to Shadow One," said the communicator. "Report back to base. The fleet can clean up from here."

"Yes sir," said Danya.

Jason watched as the assault ship began charging back down toward the planet. It broke through the atmosphere and began heading toward the mountains. The craft descended into the ravine and entered the base.

Once the cabin pressure had equalized, Jason ripped his helmet off and exited the spacecraft. The hangar was full of people and they were all cheering. Once on the floor of the hangar, Jason unzipped his G-suit and took it off, watching Danya do the same thing in front of him.

"You did us proud," said Hatshenya. "All of you did."

"Only a small victory," said Danya. "The war is far from over."

Hatshenya nodded. "I believe that you've all earned yourselves a night of celebration," she said. "Wouldn't you say so, Grand General?"

"I would definitely say so," said Sazún. "For tonight only, we celebrate the victory of the battle of Earth."

"Isn't this the time to assert ourselves on the Vazonian Empire?" asked Danya. "We have our foot on their throat. Why don't we crush them?"

Danya shook her head and walked away.

10:

I: The Queen watched as Supreme Commander Katán entered the royal chamber and knelt before her.

[What's the latest news from the Solar System?] asked the Queen.

[Your highness, the entire Vazonian fleet has been destroyed,] said the Commander. [There were no survivors.]

The Queen stood up. [You've failed in the eyes of Xiaf, Commander,] she said. [You are to be sacrificed immediately.]

[But your highness, all is not lost,] said the Commander. [The war is far from over.]

[The war is over for you,] said the Queen. [Guards, bring him to the chamber.]

[No, your highness, I beg you,] said the Commander. [Have mercy. Think of my family.]

[Yes, you've failed them too,] said the Queen. [Xiaf will be pleased with your sacrifice.]

The guards began dragging the Commander away.

II:

Jason wandered through the base. He stopped at every door he came to, looking inside and then moving on. He turned a corner and stopped at the entrance of a training room. Danya stood in front of a punching bag, beating it as viciously as she could. Jason walked up behind her.

"So this is how you celebrate a victory?" he asked. "You train harder?"

Danya spun around and kicked the punching bag. It broke off its chain and fell to the floor.

"What are you?" asked Jason. "What aren't you telling us about yourself? When did you call that woman with the eye your aunt?"

Danya ignored him and drew her pistol. She pointed it down at the punching bag and shot it. Jason covered his ears.

"What the fuck are you doing?" he asked.

Danya shot the bag again.

Jason grabbed the gun and wrenched it out of her hands, pushing her down on the ground just like she'd taught him to do. She stayed there and cried out as loudly as she could, throwing her fists down against the rock floor. Jason walked around and knelt down to look at her. There were tears in her eyes. She was crying.

"What's wrong?" he asked. "Tell me. Please tell me. I'm begging you: tell me what you're afraid of."

Danya leapt to her feet, pushing Jason to the ground. She ran away as her tears fell to the floor. Jason stood up and paused for a moment. He then left the training room, and began walking toward the cafeteria. Once there, he looked around and saw Sabenya scooping some food onto a plate. He walked up to her. She smiled.

"Good shooting up there, soldier," she said. "What a great victory for the resistance."

"Definitely," said Jason. He paused. "But we now have another problem. You say you've known Danya for a long time. How long have you known her?"

"Since she was fifteen years old," said Sabenya. "Why?"

"Because I want to figure out where she came from," said Jason. "I want to understand what horrible thing she doesn't want anyone to know about her."

"She never talked about her life before we were together with Grand General Sazún," said Sabenya. "Honestly, I've always wanted to know where she came from too. Where is she now?"

"She ran off crying after I took her gun away from her," said Jason.

"You had to take her gun from her?" asked Sabenya. "And she was crying?" Sabenya immediately put the tray down. "Let's go find her," she said.

III:
Faustemi flipped the switch and the machine came to life before him.

[Success,] he said. [The replication machine lives.]

[It's beautiful, sir,] said Konsel.

[Alert the Queen,] said Faustemi. [Her gift awaits. She will become immortal.]

Konsel hurried out of the laboratory. Faustemi looked over his creation as he waited. After a short time, the Queen walked into the laboratory.

[What is this?] asked the Queen. [How will this give me the gift?]

[This, your highness, is a replication machine,] said Faustemi. [It will create for you a new body, genetically identical to yours, but fresher and stronger. And into this new body we will encode your mind: your memories, your emotions, all things that give you your greatness.]

[Excellent,] said the Queen. [How long will this process take?]

[If we begin now, I can have your new body ready in thirty days,] said Faustemi.

[Then we will begin now,] said the Queen. [I will live on into eternity.]

[Enter the chamber, your highness,] said Faustemi. [Step inside the casing and your journey toward eternal life will begin.]

The Queen stepped inside the Chamber. Faustemi flipped the switch.

IV: General Ulysses stood at the podium before the Interstellar Council and looked down at his notes.

"So, in conclusion, the entire Vazonian fleet was destroyed," said the General. "Most significantly because our own intelligence had the vision to see the invasion coming and had the vision to recognize the existence of the Vazakanian resistance group. Intelligence gathering on our planet Earth has long been advanced beyond anything present in any other star system. And it is my firm belief that were the countries of my world to pool their resources in gathering intelligence, then we could rival the Vazonian Ven Thar. Let me ask you, the members of the Interstellar Union: do you know our enemy? Do you know how they think? Do you know how they attack and how they plan for battle?" The general nodded his head. "We on Earth now do," he said. "Which brings me to my final and most crucial point." He paused and looked over the council. "I ask you, the members of the Interstellar Council, to grant me permission to lead the Interstellar Union as the Supreme Union Commander. For the very first time in this conflict, we have managed to halt the advance of the Vazonian Empire. Ladies and gentlemen, I understand this enemy. I understand them in ways you do not and currently cannot. And as is such, I make a motion for the council to grant me full command of military operations in the Interstellar Union. I understand the politics of this decision. I understand that Earth is only single star system that is relatively new to the Union, but I ask you this: do you want to keep your freedom, or do you want to fall at the hands of the Vazonian Queen? Something must be done in the wake of this victory. I can lead us all the way to Vazakanya City and into the Royal Palace. Ladies and gentlemen of the Interstellar Union, I ask you to make the right decision. Let us move the question."

The moderator spoke into the microphone. "Do I hear a second for the Director's motion to be granted the title of Supreme Union Commander?" he asked.

"Second," said the translator of the United Nations ambassador.

"Then the council will now hold a vote," said the moderator. "Ladies and gentlemen, please vote on the Director's motion to take command of military operations for the entire Interstellar Union."

Ulysses put his hand over the microphone and turned to the President of the United States.

"This had better pass," said Ulysses. "If it doesn't, the council rarely overturns its decisions."

"It'll pass," said the President. "After the speech you gave, they don't want the U.N. Ambassador to open the floor back up for argument. They want to go home. The U.N. Ambassador seconded your motion. I know how this process works."

"True," said General Ulysses. "But if it doesn't pass, we're out of luck."

The two men waited for the results.

"By a margin of two votes, the motion passes," said the moderator. "Supreme Commander Ulysses will now command all military operations for the Interstellar Union."

"I yield the floor," said General Ulysses. "Today begins the first day of the Vazonian Empire's demise. We will take this battle to the halls of the holy city."

V: Danya stood at the edge of the cliff. It was a drop that would most definitely kill her. She stood there, staring down at the rocks below.

A voice spoke out from behind her. "What are you doing, Danya?" it asked.

Danya turned to find Grand General Sazún standing behind her. Danya said nothing.

"This will solve nothing," said Sazún. "Be at peace with yourself. It's the Vazakanian Way."

Danya remained silent. She looked down over the ledge.

Several moments passed.

"Before you jump," said Sazún. "You should know that I've always known your secret. I've always known you were the one the Queen spared and then raised as her own daughter. There was nothing you could have possibly done to avoid that fate. You were a newborn child: defenseless against the world around you. Why you feel that you're an evil person because of that is a mystery to me."

Danya took a long look down over the ledge. She closed her eyes.

The sound of footsteps could be heard behind her. "Get away from there," yelled Jason. "You're going to kill yourself over this? You're just going to end your life after all you've done to try and free the galaxy?"

Danya remained silent.

"I'm very disappointed in you then," said Jason. "If I know anything about you, I know that there is nothing you're not tough enough to handle. Get off of there. Who are you kidding? Who are you kidding by even thinking about taking the easy way out? I thought you were incapable of taking the easy way out. Is this how you want to be remembered? The deadliest fighter the galaxy has ever seen jumping to her death because she was afraid of people knowing the truth about her? She was afraid not of death, not of torture, and not of the enemy, but of the people around her judging her once they knew what she was hiding from them. If this is how you want to be remembered, then do it: jump. Go right ahead and end your life."

Danya stood still on the ledge.

"Jump," yelled Jason. "Fucking do it. You want me to start writing your eulogy or something? What the fuck are you waiting for? Fucking kill yourself and get it over with."

Danya stepped back from the ledge and collapsed to her knees, burying her face in her hands. "I love her," she screamed. It echoed across the mountain range. "I could never kill her."

There was a pause as Sazún, Sabenya, and Jason watched Danya cry.

"Danya," said Sazún. "Do you believe that you are wrong to defend the people of the galaxy from the harm your mother wishes to do to them?"

"No," yelled Danya. She shook her head and threw her fist against the ground. "She's disgraceful." Danya gasped as she cried. "But I stood there at her throne. I looked into her eyes. I watched her cry at the sight of me. I walked away. I couldn't do it."

"Why do you feel that you can't live with yourself because of this?" asked Sazún. "Why does the simple fact trouble you that you have enough compassion for the woman who raised you that you could not kill her?"

Danya said nothing.

"Of course you love your mother, Danya," said Sazún. "But you can still fight to stop all the harm she wishes to do to the galaxy."

"Since the day I left her, I've only trained to kill her," said Danya. "And it was all in vain."

"It was not in vain," said Sazún. "You're an invaluable part of this resistance. How can you say that it was all in vain?"

Danya was silent.

Jason stepped forward. He took a deep breath and sat down in front of Danya.

"Tell me," he said. "What do you want to happen to you in all of this?"

Danya shook her head. Tears fell from her eyes to the dirt.

"Let's start a little slower then," said Jason. "Let's introduce ourselves. My name is Jason Constantine. What's your name?"

Grand General Sazún motioned Sabenya to follow him. They went back into the base.

"I know you must have a name," said Jason. "What is it? It's okay. You can tell me now. You don't need to hide from us anymore. What's your name?"

Danya's voice was shaky. "Na Danya Vih Zalenya," she said. "I didn't know that until today."

"Nice to meet you then," said Jason. He paused. "I've got an idea. Everyone in the base is celebrating the victory right now. I'm sure they wouldn't mind letting us in on the celebration. After all, we were both in Shadow One."

"I can't go in there," said Danya. She shook her head. Her tears fell to the ground. "I can't do it."

"You fucking kidding me?" asked Jason. "You're afraid of people judging you? You're not afraid of dying, you're not afraid of being tortured, and you're not afraid of anything that could do you any other sort of harm, but you're afraid of answering questions about your past? Bullshit. Get up soldier. We're going in."

Jason rose to his feet in the rays of the setting sun. Danya remained on the ground for a long moment but then she stood up.

"That's the spirit," said Jason. "Let's go introduce the resistance to the Queen's daughter."

11:

I: General Ulysses exited the shuttle and walked down into the hangar. A uniformed man walked up to him and extended his hand. The two men shook hands. The Vazakanian General's grip was iron-tight.

"My name is Grand General Sazún," said the Vazakanian General. "I have commanded No Kasanosi for nine years. In my time as Grand General, we have grown from a local resistance group spread across a single star system to a vast revolutionary force that now spans across the entire Vazonian Empire and beyond. For a short time, I was your most hated enemy. Long ago, I served the Queen and I was promoted to the position of Grand General of the Vazonian Empire. While I held the position, I launched not a single attack against anyone because I felt the Queen's doctrine was unjust and fundamentally flawed. Nine years later, I stand here now determined to forge an alliance that will stand as the beginning of the Vazonian Empire's demise."

General Ulysses looked into Grand General Sazún's emerald gaze. The Grand General blinked not once.

"General Henry Ulysses," said Ulysses. "It's an honor to meet you, Grand General. Had I known of your resistance sooner, I can't help but imagine what we could have done to halt the Queen long ago."

"It is unwise to live in the past, General," said Sazún. "That is a lesson I have learned many times in my tenure as the commander of the resistance. We must think about the present and the future."

"Very true, Grand General," said Ulysses. "In the present, we have the Vazonian Empire back on its heels. What if we use this momentum we've gained to go on the offensive? The planet Issius was the launching point of the Vazonian attack. It's virtually undefended as we speak."

"The resistance presence on that world is strong," said Sazún. "If we plan this invasion together, General, the resistance giving aid and support to your troops on the ground, and your troops giving us access to better weapons and combat technology, we will be a force to be feared. It is my personal opinion that our next move should make a statement to the Queen and her military. It should let her know that the tide of this war has turned against her and it should beg the question as to what she will do about it."

General Ulysses thought for a moment. "I like the way you think, Grand General," he said. "I say that you and I collaborate to figure out how we can take Issius as loudly as possible."

"Yes," said Sazún. "It will accomplish several goals. First and foremost, it will put the Queen into a position that she is unfamiliar with, which is that of having to play defense. Before she rose to power, this woman was an outsider to the system. She was never schooled to handle the trials of war as every king and queen before her was.

She was a business executive. The empire is business. I have a hunch that she will not know what to do. It was evident as she was trying to take this planet: their invasion force did not retreat in the face of certain defeat. Every one of their warships was destroyed. All she knows it offense."

II: Danya put her hand of cards down face up on the table.

"I win again," she said. She smiled. It was a beautiful smile: the first Jason had ever seen on her face.

"You're really good at this game," said Jason. "Where did you learn to play it?"

"Played it with, well, the Queen, all the time," said Danya.

"Is she the Queen to you, or is she your mother to you?" asked Jason.

Danya was silent for a moment. "I played it with my mother all the time," said Danya. "She is my mother. She raised me to age thirteen, and that makes her my mother."

"Now, you do think what she's doing is wrong, don't you?" asked a Vazakanian man.

"I would want nothing more than to see it stop," said Danya. She paused. "But I also want to make her understand that what she's doing is wrong."

"Well good luck with that," said the Vazakanian man. "I'd love to see that happen, but I'm willing to bet it won't."

"You don't know her like I do," said Danya. She paused. "Her goal isn't to be evil." Danya shook her head. "She doesn't believe she's doing anything wrong. We all talk about her like she's consciously decided to be evil.

It's her perception of right and wrong that's the problem. She believes that her actions are justified by the fact that she saved the Vazakanian Empire from collapse. Now that I think about it, I might be able to convince her to relinquish the throne. This whole idea that the war is a matter of good and evil is not very rational. There is no one in the Vazonian Empire that believes he or she is evil and has embraced being evil. That is a fictional concept. It doesn't work with the Vazakanian Way. I'm going to try to help my mother see the error of what she's doing."

"How could you ever possibly do that?" asked Jason. "What could you possibly say to her?"

"She told me herself in our confrontation that I'm the rightful heiress of the empire," said Danya. "But she refused to give me the throne because she believed I wasn't fit for it."

"So what are you going to do then?" asked Jason.

Danya was silent for a moment. "Well, what if I proved to her that I'm fit for the throne?" she asked. "What if I prove to her that I can be a leader?"

"How would you do that?" asked Jason.

Danya nodded. "By stepping up and leading," she said. "And leading well."

"Sounds like a plan," said Jason. "It seems to me that you're figuring out who you are very quickly, although, that'll probably be a lot harder than you made it sound."

III: Faustemi read the gauges carefully, taking notes on the progress of the project.

[It works,] he said. [This will be my crowning achievement as a healer.]

[But sir,] said Konsel. [This is the forbidden science. Xiaf strictly prohibits this. It is in the sacred text.]

[Xiaf speaks to us through the Queen,] said Faustemi. [The Queen's words are the words of Xiaf.]

[But sir,] said Konsel. [Surely you cannot mistake the Queen for Xiaf. They are not one and the same.]

[Or are they?] asked Faustemi. [If the Queen becomes immortal, then does she not become one with Xiaf?]

[Your words are dangerous,] said Konsel. [There is no being equal to Xiaf.]

[Perhaps not,] said Faustemi. [But what if the Queen is of Xiaf and not for Xiaf?]

[What do you mean, sir?] asked Konsel.

[The Queen is a creation of Xiaf and is therefore part of Xiaf,] said Faustemi. [It is all a matter of perception.]

IV: Jason walked beside Danya as they came to her room. She opened the door and turned the light on.

"I like the new Danya," said Jason. "I like her a lot."

"Is she new or is she just free?" asked Danya.

"Maybe a combination of both," said Jason. "Whatever she is, I like her."

Danya smiled. Jason watched as she untied her sash, pulling her top open and taking it off. She turned away from him and dropped her top onto her bed, then sliding her skirt down to her ankles where she stepped out of it and kicked off her boots.

She sat down naked on her bed, her inner thighs held in a not-so-modest stance as she smiled at him. She looked down over her body as he gave it a good look.

"You sure you don't want a picture?" she asked. "We could make it happen."

"I told you," said Jason. "With a body like yours, it would be a picture worth framing and putting on the wall. You have a work of art for a body. That's the only way I can describe it: it's art. Everything about your body is perfect. And then now I see that you're a beautiful person on the inside too."

"Really?" asked Danya. "You think I'm beautiful on the inside?"

"Definitely," said Jason. "And it's a relief to see that beauty now. You should be proud of what you are."

Jason stepped up to the bed and sat down next to her. He looked down across her body, from her breasts to her flesh where she sat.

"You're amazing," he said. "So beautiful." He shook his head. "You really are a work of art. Take it from a man: you're a very special girl."

Danya laughed. "Is this how men in your culture talk to women they desperately want to have sex with?" she asked. "Because, if it is, it's kind of cute."

Jason opened his mouth to speak but thought better of it and said nothing.

"No, don't feel ashamed of it," said Danya. "If this is how it works in your culture, I understand. But it's very odd to me."

"I was just trying to give you a compliment," said Jason. "I think you're beautiful and now I see a beautiful person in you too."

"You tried to tell me I'm special," said Danya. She chuckled. "Vazakanian women don't go for that sort of thing. There was no sincerity behind it. The look on your face tells me exactly what your intentions are. There's a reason Vazakanian women dress the way we do. We do it because it's much easier to judge a man's intentions when he's sexually excited about us. The less a girl is wearing, the easier it is for her to see a man for what he is."

"I assure you I have more respect for you than that," said Jason.

"I didn't say you had no respect for me," said Danya. "I know you respect me. I'm just talking about your seduction methods. A Vazakanian girl can tell when your words are insincere. Your words should always match your intentions, even if all you want to do is fuck a girl. Vazakanian women actually get it: we understand how everything men do around us tends to be part of a plot to seduce us. And, don't take it personally, but we find it distasteful when a man's words don't match his intentions. You don't have to lie about wanting to have sex with us. We understand that it's just the way men are."

Jason paused. "I don't think I understand," he said. "What exactly do you mean?"

Danya shrugged her shoulders. She cupped her hands around her breasts and held them up. "What do you think of them?" she asked. "Tell me."

"You want me to tell you what I think of your breasts?" asked Jason.

"No, I want you to tell me how fucking horny they make you and I'd like you to describe to me what you'd like to do to them without sparing any detail," said Danya. "That's what I'd like to know."

"It doesn't sound very respectful to tell you that though," said Jason.

"Well, believe it or not," said Danya. "It is. It's just unbearable for me to hear you try to charm me and tell me I'm a special human being. I'm not special. I just have a body that really excites you. And I can't take you seriously if you're going to sit there and tell me I'm special. If all you want is sex, then let that be known." She looked down at her breasts. "So, what do you think?" she asked. "I think they could be smaller. It would make combat easier, at least."

Jason paused but then nodded. "Well," he said. He paused. He shook his head. "Sorry. It feels too wrong."

"It feels wrong to talk like that because it takes away your power over women," said Danya. "If you can't deceive us into allowing you to use our bodies for your satisfaction, then women have the power. Now you know how it feels to be manipulated. Kind of makes you wonder if you even deserve to have sex with me, doesn't it?"

Danya stretched her legs apart where she sat and spread her flesh with her fingertips before him. She began massaging it gently. Jason stared at the sight. He had never felt such desire in his life.

"Look, I'm sorry," said Jason. "I guess I never really thought about the way it all works before. So, if you can ever forgive me for being naïve, I would like to have sex with you sometime."

"You think you deserve to have sex with me though?" asked Danya. "Do you really think you do?"

"Well, how would I have known any better?" asked Jason. "Like you said, it's the culture I come from. Granted, I could have purer intentions, but why does a guy like me even go into the armed forces: it's to become a hero so girls will want me. I don't think there's anything I can do about that. I'm just a pervert. That's the way I am. I'm sorry. I'd gotten the impression that women in your culture were very promiscuous, and I've been dying to take advantage of that. But I'm sorry if I was wrong."

"Are you kidding?" asked Danya. "You were very right." She nodded. "Vazakanian women are very promiscuous. But we're proud of that. We embrace it." Danya nodded. "Yeah, you really wouldn't believe how warped our minds are. It makes me horny just to see the lust for me in your eyes. Women in my culture have learned to equate a man's desire with their own. The more you want us, the more we want you."

"Huh?" asked Jason. "Then what was that whole lecture about?"

"Well, that was just to make you think," said Danya. "You've obviously never thought about how you treat women you're attracted to before. Hearing you call me special was real turn off for me. It was a buzz kill. Sabenya would have done a better job lecturing you. She can really give a lecture. When she eventually seduces you, and she will, you should ask her about feminism and gender equality. There is no one in the resistance who understands it like she does. Do it after the sex though. You can't be aroused during the discussion."

"But I mean, all of those things you just said," said Jason. "They all make perfect sense. Women could empower themselves if they'd realize what I was doing to you and then decide not to stand for it."

"Yeah, of course they could," said Danya. "And they did, over seven-thousand five hundred years ago. We forced men to stop masking their intentions, but the problem was that they didn't care. So we've moved on from fighting for equality in the sense you think of it. It's not even an issue anymore. Vazakanian men and women coexist peacefully."

"How?" asked Jason.

"Both genders have accepted the fact that neither one can change the basic nature of the other," said Danya. "We're enlightened to human nature. And, curiously enough, both genders have become very comfortable with the basic nature of the other for the most part: the emotional and sensitive nature of women and the lustful and domineering nature of men: both genders have accepted it and have become at peace with it. So, thousands of years later, across our culture, you'll now find men that feel no discomfort with being sensitive and emotional, and you'll now find completely shameless women that constantly have sex on their mind and have learned to desire any man that will openly reveal lust toward them. Of course, men are now very picky about choosing sex partners. For some reason, they need to feel like they're special and not just another one of a girl's conquests."

"So, it's backwards now?" asked Jason. "Now men need to fight for their own equality?"

Danya paused. "Huh," she said. "Never thought about that. You might have a point there." She paused. She turned her head and kissed him, wrapping her arms around him and pulling him down on top of her with the bed beneath them.

"How about now?" she asked. "Will you tell me what you want to do to me now? I really want to know."

"Wow, you're fucking nasty," said Jason. "I didn't know you could be like this." He paused. "I want it to be a surprise," he said. "I won't tell you what I'm going to do to you."

"I like the sound of that," said Danya. She pushed him off to the side and sat at the end of the bed where she bunched the fingers of her right hand together and reached down to her fleshy seam, beginning to push into it. She pushed and pushed, gradually working her hand in past her knuckles further and further until it was wrist-deep inside herself. She smiled at him as she felt around inside her own flesh, plunging her fist in and out again and again. Jason raised his eyebrows as he watched.

"I can always see it in your eyes," she said. "I can see it now."

"What can you see?" asked Jason. He continued to stare at her submerged hand as she continued to work it through her flesh. Danya smiled as he stared.

"Taste it for me," she said. "Tell me how it tastes."

Jason nodded his head. He began licking the flesh around her now-buried hand. It was so smooth and warm. It was amazing. She pulled her hand out as he did it. He continued licking her flesh after the hand came out. He sucked on it hard. It tasted heavenly. She groaned as he sucked on her clit. It was so, so soft. After a moment, he pulled back and stared down at her breasts. They were the most perfect breasts he had ever seen in his life: so large and round with a slight comfortable sag. He wanted them. He reached out, cupping his hands around them and caressing them gently in his palms, massaging them softly like a fantasy come true. They were silky smooth like a dream. She brought her hands up behind his head, pulling him down to her lips where she began kissing him. He squeezed her breasts as she kissed him.

Jason pulled back and brought his head down to her breasts, licking them both and sucking on them as he did so. He pulled back and nodded as he licked his lips.

"Tasty?" asked Danya. "I have good flavor, don't I?"

"You're very sweet and spicy," said Jason. "Should be a candy flavor."

She pulled his shirt off. He took his pants and underwear off as well before pushing her down beneath him on the bed. He licked her breasts some more and then pulled back, pushing her legs back against her shoulders and reaching down with his hands to spread her seam apart. Jason drew his tongue across the pink flesh within again and again. He could not get enough. He sucked on her clit hard again and she groaned. He kissed her flesh. He kissed it twice before pulling back and staring down at it in awe.

He deepened his fingers into her depth and pulled it open as far as it would go. He was amazed by how much he could stretch it. It was very elastic. He nodded his head and bunched the fingers of his own right hand together, guiding them between her seam and then pushing. He pushed and twisted back and forth, gradually working his hand into her depth deeper and deeper. He worked it and worked it until it was wrist-deep into her flesh.

Danya gasped and groaned as he curiously felt around inside her there, twisting his hand back and forth against her inner flesh. It felt amazing on his hand. It was warm and wet like a fleshy cloud comforting him. He gently caressed her right breast with his free hand as he massaged her most tender flesh with his thumb.

"You're a depraved man," said Danya. She breathed in and exhaled as he strained against her most tender flesh. "You know how a Vazakanian girl likes to be treated."

Jason clenched his hand into a fist within her and began working her as hard as he could, wrenching and twisting his knuckles back and forth hard over the same spot again and again. She cried out as he did it. She squealed.

Jason continued to work her. His arm began to get tired as he worked, but he pushed on. Her flesh was so soft and wet on his hand.

"So hard," she said. "So, so hard." She gasped again and massaged herself with her fingertips. Her eyes rolled back into her head.

A geyser of wet warmth erupted out of her flesh as it began clamping again and again around his hand. Jason pulled his fist out and Danya grabbed his head, pushing his face down into the surge. He opened his mouth and gulped it down. He pulled back and just watched as it pulsed up into the air and rained down on them both. It died away. Jason kissed her flesh again.

Danya smiled at him. "Don't hold back," she said.

Jason fell on top of her and plunged his length into her depth as deep as it could go, beginning to wrench it back and forth within her. It felt so good: it was beyond words. She groaned as he worked. He had never been more aroused in his life. It was the softest, warmest, and most comforting feeling he had ever felt. The flesh of her depth was a soft heaven around him. It was so warm, and so wet, and so comforting. He could feel it so wet and soothing as it slid against him. He picked up the pace, working her so hard that it shook the bed. She cried out.

"Harder," she said. She gasped. "Work it."

Jason began going as fast and as hard as he could. It was a wet sensual heaven slipping again and again against his flesh. His dream was coming true. Her body was the long-desired object of his lust. It was now his. And it was so warm, so soft, so deep; it abruptly began clamping down around him as if swallowing him. It was overwhelming.

He pulled out of her and knelt over her chest. He held himself in his right hand and released over her breasts.

It was a beautiful ecstasy of sensual heaven coursing through him. He slowed down and savored the moment as he covered her curves with his passion. It was as if all of his dreams had come true. It was incredible. He drenched her breasts with his passion. He pulled back as his pleasure died away and watched as her own flesh continued to erupt as if it were a fountain. He spread her seam apart and sucked on it. The wet warmth flooded into his mouth. It tasted like a dream. He gulped it down as it died away. Once it had, Danya exhaled, sitting up on the bed and beginning to lick his passion off of her own breasts just as he'd envisioned it.

"I could get used to this," said Jason. "I really could."

"Yeah, not bad for a girl that hasn't had sex in seven years or so," said Danya. "You know, they say that Vazakanian women are addictive to men that aren't used to them."

"Why do they say that?" asked Jason.

"The fact of the matter is that Vazakanians are all genetically modified to be as attractive as possible," said Danya. "Starting in the sixty-two fifties, we had the technology to genetically enhance ourselves. The government decided to let the free mearket decide if it was ethical to let parents control how their children would look." She paused. "A thousand years later, you won't find an unattractive Vazakanian. In the Vazonian Empire now, the study of genetics is the 'forbidden science.'"

"I didn't know that," said Jason. "So what do Vazakanians naturally look like?"

"We've forgotten," said Danya. "No one can say for sure. It's one of the mysteries of our civilization. We know what Queen Vazakanya herself looked like. She looked the way every Vazakanian woman looks now: blonde hair, green eyes, full breasts, and taller than the average woman in just about every other human civilization. I guess you could say that, because I'm actually descended from her, my appearance is probably more natural than it is for every other Vazakanian woman."

"Is that good or bad?" asked Jason.

"Did you enjoy that purely lustful experince?" asked Danya. "I know I did."

"More than any sex I've ever had in my life," said Jason.

"It was just the will of the free market," said Danya. "Make of it whatever you want. The free market isn't good or evil. It's simply a system for progress. But the progress depends on how the free market is regulated. Regulate it too much, and progress goes nowhere. But if there is no regulation and no governing body to make the free market accountable when it goes astray, then we find ourselves in the midst of a Galactic War."

V: General Ulysses stood at the podium before the Interstellar Council.

"This was a devastating defeat for the Vazonian Empire," he said. "They sent to Earth a fleet of over five hundred warships. None survived the battle. Their attack was launched from the Alpha Centauri System, but their fleet was drawn from the occupied Issius System. The absence of these five hundred warships in the Issius System leaves the planet virtually undefended as we speak. I make a motion that we now go on the offensive and liberate Issius immediately. If we can do this, then we will have the Vazonian Empire back on its heels."

The moderator spoke. "Do I hear a second for the General's motion to attack the Vazonian occupation forces at Issius?" he asked.

There was silence. But then one of the representatives seconded the motion.

"Very well, then the council will now vote," said the moderator.

The General waited anxiously as the council voted.

"The motion passes by a unanimous vote," said the moderator. "The Union will invade Issius."

"Thank you ladies and gentlemen," said General Ulysses. "I yield the floor."

Ulysses walked away.

Part II:

1:

I: Danya sat in the interrogation room as General Hatshenya questioned her.

"So you know all three of the master clearance codes?" asked Hatshenya.

"Yes," said Danya. "There were three doors you had to go through if you wanted access to my section of the palace. The codes the servants used would change frequently, but the master codes always worked."

"Could you give us those codes?" asked Hatshenya. "They would be very helpful to us. I'm sure you would agree."

"All three of them are sixteen digits long," said Danya. "I'd need to be standing in front of a keypad to do it."

"That can be arranged," said Hatshenya. "Do you need a standard nine digit keypad?"

"Yes, ma'am," said Danya. "If you put me in front of one, then I'll remember what I'm supposed to press."

Hatshenya spoke into her communicator. "I need a nine-digit keypad," she said. "Immediately. Thank you." Hatshenya looked up at Danya again. "So what was your relationship with her like?" asked Hatshenya. "Were you very close to her?"

"She was always very busy," said Danya. "But in the time I did spend with her, she would read me stories, we would play games, and she'd tell me she loved me."

"What was it that made you decide to run away?" asked Hatshenya.

"I walked in on a sacrifice," said Danya. "I went to a part of the palace I wasn't supposed to go to. I watched her torture and mutilate a man. I ran to my room as fast as I could. I found a servant there cleaning my room. She asked me why I was crying so I told her what I'd seen. The servant immediately locked the door and told me that my mother was a murderer. The servant told me that I was young and it wasn't too late to save myself from becoming what my mother was. The servant helped me write a suicide note and she helped me escape from the palace. She told me never to tell anyone who I was."

The door to the room opened and a lieutenant walked inside with a keypad. He put it on the table.

"Thank you, lieutenant," said Hatshenya. She looked at Danya. "Can you go slow so I can record the codes?"

"Yes, ma'am," said Danya. Danya looked down at the keypad and thought for a moment. "This was the first door," she said. She began inputting the code into the keypad. She closed her eyes as she went along. Once she finished, she opened them.

"You're sure that's the correct code?" asked Hatshenya.

"Positive," said Danya. "Now this was the second door."

Danya punched in another code. Hatshenya recorded it.

"The third door," said Danya. "I would decorate. It depended on the season." She nodded her head. She closed her eyes and input the code.

"Thank you, Danya," said Hatshenya. "Can you think of anything else that might help us win this war?"

"I was only thirteen years old, ma'am," said Danya. "It shocks me that the three codes are the master clearance codes for the entire empire. I didn't know I was that important to her."

"Then you're dismissed," said Hatshenya. "Thank you for helping us, Danya. I know this must be very difficult for you."

"Ma'am," said Danya. "I want to try and convince her to relinquish the throne to me."

Hatshenya was silent for a moment. "What makes you think it would be worth trying?" she asked.

"Because she told me that I was the rightful heiress of the empire," said Danya. "But she refused to give me the throne because she felt I wasn't fit to be Queen. I want to prove to her that I am fit to be Queen."

"How could you possibly do that?" asked Hatshenya.

"I'm the remaining one," said Danya. "No Kasanosi was born of the hope that someday the remaining one could save the empire. I'm the rightful Queen."

"If the Queen were to suddenly relinquish the throne to you," said Hatshenya, "then what would you do?"

"I'd dissolve the Vazonian Empire," said Danya. "And I'd form a council of Vazakanians to rewrite the constitution. We would take to mind the mistakes of the first Vazakanian Empire. We would leave nothing unclear or unaccounted for, and once we'd enacted the constitution, I would declare the period of martial law to be over and I would give the power back to the people."

"That sounds like a very rational idea," said Hatshenya. She paused. "Do you know where I came from, Danya? Do you know how I came to the resistance?"

"No, ma'am," said Danya. "You never told me."

"I was the last Vazakanian King's political advisor," said Hatshenya. "That was my title. But the reality was that he was old and weak and I had to look after him much like a caregiver. Toward the end of the Empire, I was the one responsible for all he was trying to do to save the Empire from ruin. I was the one trying to unite it and give it strength through the Vazakanian Way. I did everything I could to make him seem strong and charismatic in his appearances and speeches, but the truth was that he hardly knew where he was half the time. His mind was gone."

"I never knew this, Ma'am," said Danya. "You must have been very young to be in that position."

"I was in my thirties," said Hatshenya. "I was appointed to the position when it was mostly symbolic: the Vazakanian Empire was as prosperous as ever at that time. But then the crisis and the depression hit, and I found myself having to learn my position as I went along. I tried so hard to make the King seem strong." Hatshenya shook her head. "In hindsight, I wonder what would have happened had I been the one to step up and try to unite the empire myself. The heir to the throne was still too young for the responsibility of being the next King. Under the Vazakanian Constitution, that was what the royal family was for: to provide the people with a comforting source of inspiration to be strong and to be proud of their heritage in a time of crisis. For many years after the fall of the Vazakanian Empire, I blamed myself. I thought the Vazonian Empire was my fault. But Grand General Sazún brought me to my senses once he joined the resistance. Before he arrived, I had been commanding it. A Vazakanian woman never likes to relinquish her power to a man, but, sometimes, greatness knows no gender. In only nine years, the Grand General has done what I could have only dreamed of doing."

"I had no idea," said Danya. "I had no idea you were right in the middle of it."

"But what I'm saying, Danya," said Hatshenya, "is that it's never wise to blame yourself for problems that are vastly greater than yourself. And I want you to remember this."

II: "The people of Issius are desperate for liberation," said Sazún. "I've had the resistance scout the sentiment toward the Queen. Publicly, they wouldn't dare speak out against her, but privately, they despise her."

"Would it be possible for your resistance to fuel the flames of this sentiment?" asked General Ulysses. "Spreading rumors, circulating flyers, doing anything to grow the anti-Vazonian sentiment?"

"That, General, is what we do," said Sazún. "That is how we recruit our fighters."

"Then let's say you intensify your campaign on Issius," said General Ulysses. "Give the people hope: spread the news of our victory here and our new alliance. Make them believe that the tide of this war is turning and that they could be very close to freedom."

"That alone would not convince them that they could be close to freedom," said Sazún. "The decision to defy the will of Xiaf is not easy. It is not simply defying the will of a Queen. It is making a decision to take control of your own life."

There was a pause.

"You have any celebrities in your resistance?" asked General Ulysses. "Anyone famous?"

"We have the Queen's only daughter," said Sazún. "Commander Danya. She was Shadow One during the battle."

"The Queen's only daughter?" asked General Ulysses. "The Queen has a daughter? And she's fighting for you?"

"She has only recently admitted to being her daughter," said Sazún. "I have always known this about her, but I chose not to confront her until she was ready. She is our deadliest fighter. I would bet that there is no man or woman alive that could best her save for Director Zerpanya of Ven Thar."

"So, all this time, you had the Queen's own flesh and blood on your side and you told no one about it?" asked General Ulysses.

"The circumstances did not permit me to speak of it," said Sazún. "Her mind was very fragile. We're now doing our best to make her at peace with her identity."

"I imagine it would be difficult to live with the fact that your mother is a murderer," said General Ulysses.

"Indeed," said Sazún. "At the moment, she is in the process of finding herself."

"I hope she finds herself soon," said General Ulysses. "What an asset she could be to our cause."

"She's being helped with the companionship of your very own soldier," said Sazún. "Jason. The two of them are very close."

"Constantine?" asked General Ulysses. "And the Queen's daughter? How close are they?"

"Close enough to trust each other," said Sazún. "Were it not for your soldier, she would have ended her own life."

"How do they communicate?" asked General Ulysses. "Does she speak English?"

"We all do," said Sazún. "The language is taught to everyone that joins us."

"Why?" asked General Ulysses. "Why English?"

"In order to base our operations off of this planet," said Sazún. "We were required to first be able to go unnoticed among the people here while we constructed the base and equipped it with all of the technology that allows us to operate. We chose English simply because the American accent comes naturally to speakers of the Vazakanian Language. So, to answer your question, your soldier and Danya communicate in English."

"I see," said General Ulysses. He paused. "Let me ask you, Grand General: how do your fighters train? What facilities do they use?"

"We do not have the facilities of a conventional military outfit," said Sazún. "We are forced to improvise."

"What if," said General Ulysses, "I could have the US Military set up better training facilities for your fighters? I don't doubt their skills, but I would like to see everyone fulfill their potential."

"I would amend that offer," said Sazún. "In return for access to your training facilities, I offer to teach your fighters in the ways of Kano-Vunto."

"What's Kano-Vunto, Grand General?" asked Sazún. "A religion?"

"No, General," said Sazún. "Kano-Vunto is the Vazonian fighting style. If your people wish to fight our common enemy effectively, you must learn how they fight."

Ulysses paused. "I accept your offer," he said.

III:
[The base is on Earth,] said Zerpanya. [In the Himalayan Mountain range. Unfortunately, the Interstallar Union is now committed to protecting the resistance, so in order to destroy it, we must carry out a covert series of operations. We must scout the area to determine where to launch our attack from and we must insert operatives into the base in order to obtain a schematic of its interior.] Zerpanya looked at the hand-selected operative before her. He stood in the shadows. His face could not be seen. [You are among the most skilled agents we have in Ven Thar,] she said. [And your appearance is such that you look nothing like one of us. I am entrusting you with this mission under my leadership. The first order of business is to infiltrate the United States Planetary Defense Force. You will go to the base and give us intelligence on their operations.]

IV:
Jason put his hand of cards down on the table.

"I think I lost," he said. "I'm not sure what this one means."

"That means you won," said Sabenya. "You won everything. That's the Shadenya Card."

"Just a case of beginners luck then," said Jason. "I have no idea what I'm doing."

"You'll get the hang of it," said a Vazakanian man. "It takes time."

"What's your name again?" asked Jason.

"I'm Tofán," said the Vazakanian man. "Nu Tofán Vih Maván."

Jason nodded. "I think I'm starting to figure this out," he said. He looked at Sabenya. "So you must be Na Sabenya Vih something, right?"

"Na Sabenya Vih Moradonya," said Sabenya.

"So every Vazakanian has a Nu or a Na and Vih," said Jason. "Now what does it all mean?"

"The Na in my name means I'm female," said Sabenya. "Sabenya is my name, the Vih means of, and Moradonya is my house name."

"What's a house name?" asked Jason.

"My family name," said Sabenya. "Moradonya: like a surname in your culture."

"So my name is Jason Constantine," said Jason. "And my middle name is Edward. You don't have middle names."

"What does your name mean?" asked Tofán.

"In America, we name people based on how the name sounds to us," said Jason. "We don't even think about what the names mean for the most part."

"You don't?" asked Sabenya. "So your name doesn't mean anything but it sounds good to your people?"

"Well, it could have meaning," said Jason. "But my parents didn't think about meaning when they named me." He paused. "So what does Danya's name mean?"

"Na Danya Vih Zalenya," said Sabenya. "Danya is a name derived from the Darshakwan language. The word danya means pride, but she doesn't get the name from the meaning of the word. It's just a traditional royal name."

"What does Zalenya mean?" asked Jason.

"That's a color," said Tofán. "Any surname that's a color in our culture is a very historic surname. It dates all the way back to the beginning of the empire. Zalenya is green: the house of nature's beauty. Danya is a direct descendent of Queen Vazakanya herself."

"And Queen Vazakanya is what your people are named after, right?" asked Jason.

"She was the founder of the Empire," said Sabenya. "United the capital planet and gave us our identity."

"So she was a woman," said Jason. He paused. "I notice that there are a lot more Vazakanian women in the resistance than Vazakanian men."

"Vazakanian women don't have the rights they once had," said Sabenya. "Xiaf commands that we serve men like slaves. We really don't like that."

"What about the Queen?" asked Jason.

"The Queen serves Xiaf," said Sabenya. "Xiaf is her master. It's a double standard. The two most powerful people in the empire are women: Director Zerpanya and the Queen, even though they supposedly believe that women are supposed to be slaves to men."

V: Faustemi read the monitors and meters carefully, recording all of the data in the log book.

"How goes the progress, sir?" asked Konsel.

"Progression status is normal," said Faustemi. "We're ahead of schedule. We can complete the transition within a matter of days."

"I pray to Xiaf that there will be no setbacks," said Konsel. "For a moment, we will hold the life of the Queen in our hands."

"Xiaf will guide us," said Faustemi. "I am certain that Xiaf will protect her."

VI:
Grand General Sazún stood beside General Hatshenya as they looked over the profiles before them.

"We need two more fighters to send to the USPDF," said Sazún.

There was a pause. "Perhaps we can send Commander Danya and Lance Corporal Constantine," said Hatshenya. "Constantine is familiar with the customs of the US military. He can introduce our fighters to their ways."

"I do not know about Commander Danya," said Sazún. "She is at a very uncertain time in her life."

"I suggest her, not only because she can teach Kano-Vunto faster than anyone else, but also because Constantine will be there," said Hatshenya. "She finds comfort in his presence."

"True," said Sazún. He paused. "Very well. We will send both of them."

"I will gather them all now," said Hatshenya. "We will send them over tomorrow."

2:

I: The transport vessel touched down on the USPDF landing pad, equalizing the cabin pressure and lowering the boarding ramp. Everyone in the transport rose and filed out onto the pavement. The familiar face of General Ulysses stood there waiting. Jason and Danya stepped forward to meet him. The General stared at Danya for a moment, looking over her sparsely dressed body before nodding.

"Constantine," said General Ulysses. "I see you've chosen to return to us."

"Only to help teach you how to fight," said Jason. "Consider me an ambassador for these people. I'm going to help you understand them." He glanced at Danya. "This, sir, is the deadliest fighter you will ever meet in your lifetime. Her name is Commander Danya. Danya, this is General Ulysses."

"You're the Queen's daughter," said Ulysses.

"Yes," said Danya. "I'm her adopted daughter. She adopted me after she killed my real family."

"I'm anxious then to see just how skilled you are," said General Ulysses. He paused, looking at the pistol holstered just beneath the left side of her left breast. "Now, before I introduce you all to my troops, I would like you to understand that we do things very differently here in the United States Armed Forces. I'm sure you understand."

"Of course," said Danya. "All military outfits have their own way of operating."

"Then I must ask that you hand over any weapons you may have brought with you," said General Ulysses. "Please."

The General and Danya stared each other down for a moment, but then Danya un-holstered her pistol and handed it to General Ulysses.

"I can see we have a lot of work to do," said Danya. "Your idea of a weapon is very narrow-minded, General."

"How so, Commander?" asked General Ulysses.

Danya nodded, "What is a weapon, General, if not a device that can be used to do damage? This firearm: is it a weapon if one lacks the knowledge to use it properly? A weapon is simply a tool one uses. I can find a way to use anything as a weapon: your hat: I could kill you with it before you could blink."

"I wouldn't doubt that, Commander," said General Ulysses. "I'm sure you have knowledge of firearms, knives, swords: all sorts of weapons."

"Swords?" asked Danya. "We do not use swords in Kano-Vunto. They're impractical."

"Nonetheless," said General Ulysses. "I'm not worried about disarming you in the name of safety. I'm worried about the psychological impact of my men seeing you walk the complex with a firearm always by your side. Far more people are capable of using a firearm as a weapon than are capable of using other objects I'm sure you're trained to use."

Danya paused for a moment, but then nodded. "Understood, General," she said. "So what are your plans for us?"

"Each of your fighters will be assigned to a unit," said General Ulysses. "I have units from all across the Interstellar Union here to learn your fighting style. Your leaders, which I'm assuming are you two, will visit each unit every day to ensure that the training is going as planned."

"Sounds like a plan, General," said Danya. "Now where will we be staying?"

A bus approached the landing pad. It came to a stop behind the General.

"This bus will take you to your barracks," said General Ulysses. "I'm sure Constantine can show you all of our facilities and mess halls."

"Yes, sir," said Jason. "Everyone, follow me."

He motioned everyone to follow him onto the bus. The fighters all filed onto the bus and it began driving. It took them to a civilian area of the base. The bus came to a stop and let everyone off. A two-star general stood waiting at the entrance to the barracks.

"Welcome, No Kasanosi," he said. "We'll need to search all of your luggage before we let it into the building, but you can all go in and make yourselves comfortable."

Jason led everyone into the building. The other fighters continued to the rooms, but Danya stopped to look at the television in the common room.

"What's this monitor for?" she asked.

"I'll show you," said Jason. He picked up the remote control and turned the television on. The scene was a soap opera. Jason watched as Danya stared at the screen. Jason laughed. "You like it?" he asked.

"What is it?" asked Danya.

"It's entertainment," said Jason. "Looks like Ramón just discovered that Jessica is his sister."

Danya continued to stare at the screen.

"Have a seat," said Jason. "Let's find something good to watch."

Danya sat down on one of the couches and Jason sat down next to her. He changed the channel to a movie channel.

"Oh, this is a classic," said Jason. "It's all about the Samurai of Japan. Made every kid of my generation want to learn how to sword fight."

"Sword fight," said Danya. "More swords. Do your people have a fascination with swords?"

"No," said Jason. "Well, I'm sure some people do, but we're more about guns than swords. Why do you ask?"

"I never cared for swords," said Danya. "Like I said: they're impractical."

"I'm sure you'd know how to fight with a sword," said Jason. He changed the channel. "Nineteen seventy-two," he said. "The fist of the trilogy that shouldn't have been a trilogy. It romanticized the life of organized crime."

"Who's that?" asked Danya.

"That's Vito," said Jason. "Don't refuse his offers."

"So is that what this entertainment monitor is all about?" asked Danya. "Fighting and killing?"

Jason sighed. "Let's just go figure out where we'll be staying," he said. He rose from his seat and walked down the hallway. There was only one room left.

"What's that sound?" asked Danya. "It's coming from the wall."

"That's indoor plumbing," said Jason. "Want to go take a shower?"

"I haven't taken a shower since I was seventeen years old," said Danya. "I'd love to feel clean for once."

"Let's go find it," said Jason. He led Danya through the hallways to the showering stations. Many of the soldiers had already found them.

II:

The Queen paced back and forth across the assembly table.

[Your new orders are to seek and destroy all members of the resistance,] she said. [You will take no prisoners and you will accept no surrender.]

[How will we gain intelligence on them if we can no longer interrogate them?] asked one of the generals.

[You will do as I say,] said the Queen. [The resistance has been given enough chances to surrender to Xiaf. They are now a force to be reckoned with and we will crush them where they stand.]

A man wearing a white lab coat spoke. [Your highness,] he said. [I have joined the assembly today to inform you of a new weapon we have in development. It is still in the early stages of testing, but we may be able to adopt the use of this weapon as a new strategy.]

The Queen looked at the man. He had thick glasses.

[Continue, Doctor Himlen,] she said. [You are assigned to the research and development department of the high-energy weapons brand if am not mistaken.]

[You are not mistaken, your highness,] said the doctor. [I bring to you news of a new sort of weapon, a weapon that could potentially crush the resistance and the Interstellar Union once and for all. If you would give us a contract, we would be honored.]

[What weapon do you speak of, doctor?] asked the Queen.

[We call it the Tempest, your highness,] said the doctor. [As with the great storm of faith in Xiaf that will finally purge the galaxy of filth and lewdness. It is my personal belief that the Tempest begins with this weapon.]

[Those are bold words coming from a man of such an obscure brand of the great business we run,] said the Queen. [Tell me, doctor, what could this weapon possibly do that would be worth our precious time?]

[It can destroy an entire enemy fleet of warships,] said Himlen. [Or by simply increasing the size of the weapon, it could destroy all civilization on an inhabited planet.]

The room fell silent. The Queen laughed. [So you've created some sort doom device,] she said. [I've seen this out of brands like yours hundreds of times before. Your creations are neither reliable, nor cost-efficient, nor practical in the pace of modern warfare. They rarely work as planned, if utilized, they would bankrupt the empire, and they're too large and complicated to be transported quickly.]

[Yes, your highness,] said Himlen. [And this has all been taken into consideration with this latest design.] He held up a foam sphere. [This is your weapon,] he said. [Observe it: a simple sphere that will be made of inexpensive materials.] Himlen held up a second foam sphere with thumb tacks pressed into it. [And covering this sphere, we have these smaller objects. These smaller objects are simple thermonuclear warheads. A pair of retro-rockets causes the sphere to begin rotating in space. A timer simultaneously releases each of the warheads at precisely the same moment, and they detonate together, releasing a storm of thermonuclear energy, the likes of which no one has ever seen. Your highness, this weapon could destroy entire enemy fleets, entire enemy worlds, all very efficiently. It will be the end of the Union and the resistance.]

The room was silent. [Intriguing,] said the Queen. [If what you say is true, then I must look upon this weapon myself. You will create a prototype and you will test it. I give to you a preliminary contract. I will arrange a fleet of obsolete warships to be placed in orbit around the Biki System. If your weapon works, then we will look into using it.]

III: Jason kissed Danya as he lay in bed with her, his hands massaging her breasts gently as he did so.

"Now I'm being sincere," he said. "You really are amazing. I've never met anyone like you in my entire life."

"Don't see how you could have," said Danya. "How many girls do you know that have a Queen as their mother?"

"Can't say I know any," said Jason. He paused. "How do you think your mother feels about you now?"

"She's convinced that I've lost my way and that I'll come crawling back to her soon," said Danya. "She thinks I'll want her to be my mother again."

"You make it sound like she has no problem with you following the Vazakanian Way and lifestyle," said Jason.

"I'm guessing she thinks it's something I'll get over as I grow older," said Danya. "She once followed the Vazakanian Way and lifestyle too. Before she found Xiaf, she was a good Vazakanian."

Jason licked her breasts and sucked on them. He pulled back and kissed her again.

"You know what?" he asked. "I think I'm starting to fall in love with you."

"You do?" asked Danya. "Why? I don't know if I could ever love you, or anyone. I don't know if I'm capable of love."

There was silence.

"Do you care about me?" asked Jason. "At all?"

"Of course I do," said Danya. "But I don't love you. I just like to have you in my bed."

Jason paused. He sighed. "You're still afraid of letting me in," he said. "Trusting me, aren't you?"

"No," said Danya. "I just don't think I could ever love anyone. So let's not get too caught up in our feelings. We have to get up early tomorrow."

IV: Faustemi knelt before the Queen.

[The process is complete, your highness,] he said. [We can now transform you.]

The Queen rose from the throne. [Excellent,] she said. [It will be done now. Bring me to the chamber.]

[At once, your highness,] said Faustemi. He rose and led the Queen through the palace to the laboratory. A lifeless female body lay suspended in a chamber.

[That is my face,] said the Queen. [When I was young. That is the face I long to have once again.]

Faustemi opened the door to a small chamber. [Step inside, your highness,] he said. [This machine will transfer your mind to your new and enhanced form.]

The Queen stepped inside the chamber. Faustemi closed the door.

[Konsel,] he said. [Prepare for the transformation.]

[Yes, sir,] said Konsel. He went to work.

Faustemi went up to a control console and flipped a number of switches. [Preparing for transformation,] he said. [In three, two, one, initiate.]

He flipped another switch. The lights in the laboratory dimmed in a power surge. After a moment, the eyes of the body in the chamber opened.

[Success,] yelled Faustemi. [Konsel, drain incubation fluid. Free the Queen.]

The fluid in the chamber began to drain. Faustemi watched as the new Queen ripped the life support out of her body. The glass chamber rose into the ceiling and the Queen stepped down onto the floor of the laboratory, her wet naked body dripping as she looked over herself.

[I feel stronger,] she said. [Much stronger.]

[I have enhanced your body in many ways,] said Faustemi.

[Am I immortal?] asked the Queen. [Is there anything that could bring my existence to an end?]

[In the event of death, a copy of your mind will be saved onto a small memory chip,] said Faustemi. [Which can be recovered easily. We can then load your mind from the chip into a new body.]

The Queen nodded. [Excellent,] she said. [Xiaf will be proud to hear of your work. Fetch me a robe. I wish to go before the people to speak of my new gift.]

[At once, your highness,] said Faustemi. He paused. [What of your original body?]

The Queen thought for a moment. [Keep it fresh,] she said. [Do not dispose of it.]

3:

I: Danya watched as the soldiers trained in the ways of Kano-Vunto.

"That soldier over there," said Danya. "He seems to be getting the hang of this much faster than anyone else in the unit."

"I agree," said Jason. "It seems to come naturally to him."

Danya walked toward the unit, stepping up to the fighter she'd assigned to train it.

"What's that soldier's name over there?" she asked. "The one who seems to be catching onto this?"

"Private First Class Joe Smith," said the instructor. "Been doing a great job."

Danya watched as the outstanding soldier sparred with another soldier. The other soldier was no match for Smith.

"Very impressive," said Danya. She walked up to Smith.

"You impress me, Private," she said. "I would like you to try to kill me."

"Kill you, ma'am?" asked Smith. "You'd like me to try to kill you?"

"Yes," said Danya. "Right now."

Smith spun around and kicked at her. She grabbed his leg and directed his momentum to the ground. He quickly jumped to his feet and began throwing punches at her, backing her up toward the wall.

She made her move, catching his fist and throwing him face down on the floor. She placed her boot over his neck.

"Eighteen seconds," said the Drill Sergeant. Danya removed her foot from the man's neck and extended her hand downward to help him up. She looked into his eyes as she helped him up. They were blue.

"Impressive, Private," said Danya. "Few people can last that long against me. Keep up the good work."

"Yes, ma'am," said Smith. "I look forward to fighting you again sometime."

II: Zerpanya sat at the head of the table.

[What is the latest on the resistance?] she asked.

[It appears that Sazún has appointed his best fighters to train Union soldiers in the ways of Kano-Vunto,] said one of the men at the table. Part of his right ear was missing.

[Interesting, General Yadén,] said Zerpanya. [This would be in an effort to better equip the Union in fighting back against us, I assume.]

[It would seem as such,] said General Yadén. [The princess is overseeing the training.]

[Her skills as a fighter are second only to my own,] said Zerpanya. [She is a formidable opponent. The

Queen's orders are to take her alive should we ever encounter her again. It's a shame. I would love to have the honor of killing her myself.] Zerpanya paused. [We can only imagine what she could have been for the Vazonian Empire, but she chose not to follow that path.]

III: The Queen stood on the balcony over Vazakanya City Square as she addressed the hundreds of thousands of people.

[We are one empire, one civilization, one society,] she said. [We are the Vazonian race: faithful servants of our Lord Xiaf, the Lord who sees all and knows all and guides us. People of the Vazonian Empire, I speak before you to deliver news of a blessing from Xiaf. I, your Great Queen, Xiaf's most faithful servant, have been granted the gift of immortality. It is a blessing that will unite us. It is a blessing that will guide us. In the name of Xiaf, we live on, we fight on, we will prosper for all eternity. The Vazonian Empire is unstoppable.]

IV: Doctor Himlen looked up at the completed prototype. He nodded his head.

[I name it,] he said, [the Tempest. So begins the dawn of the Tempest.] He turned to a second scientist. [Inform the Queen. She must look upon the prototype herself. She will witness the great storm of faith in Xiaf for herself.]

Himlen stepped up to the device and looked at each thermonuclear warhead symmetrically placed on the sphere.

[The beauty,] he said. [The beauty of the end as it lies within sight. I can see it in my mind.] he turned to the second scientist again. [Can you see it, Doctor Pawnsan? This is the end of the war, this is the beginning of peace for a better galaxy, a Vazonian galaxy: a galaxy that lives to serve the will of Xiaf.]

[I can see it, sir,] said Pawnsan. [It is beautiful.]

[What will you do, Pawnsan?] asked Himlen. [What will you do in the time of peace: once the stormy skies of the Tempest have cleared and there will be nothing left to do but live in peace?]

There was a pause. [I do not know, sir,] said Pawnsan. [What will there be to do?]

[What do you mean, Pawnsan?] asked Himlen. [We will be free to do as Xiaf bids us however we please.]

V: General Ulysses sat at the table with all of the other Union Generals.

"The operation will be called Operation Shift," said General Ulysses. "It will be called Operation Shift to represent the shift in momentum from them to us. As you all know, we are currently training all Union forces in the combat style of our enemy under the guidance of our new ally in the resistance. Once our troops have been thoroughly trained in the art of fighting the Vazonian Empire, then we'll hit 'em hard and we'll hit 'em fast. We will liberate the occupied system of Issius. As we speak, Grand General Sazún of the resistance has begun a massive campaign of spreading hope to all of the people of Issius. They are beginning to crave freedom more than they ever have before. Are there any questions so far?"

"How do we know we can trust this resistance?" asked one of the other generals.

"General Darius," said General Ulysses. "In war, there are some risks you have to take if you want to win. And this risk is one we have to take. The resistance is providing us with intelligence we could never possibly gather, a window into the mind of our enemy from the point of view of those who live among them, and most of all, experience in fighting a common enemy. Trust me, General, they hate the Vazonian Empire more than we do. They fight to win back their freedom. We fight to keep ours. We have not learned what it is to live under the rule of the Queen."

"I hope you're right about them, General," said General Darius. "I would hate to see us compromised because of this alliance."

"It's a risk we have to take," said General Ulysses. He paused. "So we will launch the liberation campaign in two phases. The first phase will be to send in a combined fleet of resistance and Union warships. Having the resistance by our side provides us with far more firepower and personnel than we once had. We can now hold back a reserve fleet, one which we can send in should the initial wave need reinforcements. This is our plan so far. I plan on launching our campaign within five days."

VI: Jason sat across from Danya in the mess hall as they ate their dinner.

"So what kinds of things did you eat when you were living with the Queen?" asked Jason. "Just curious."

Danya looked away from him. "It was the best food the people could buy for me," she said. "The freshest cuts of meat, the most exotic delicacies: if it was expensive and indulgent, I ate it."

"You're still not quite comfortable about this, are you?" he asked. "You're still ashamed."

"What am I ashamed of?" asked Danya.

"Who you are," said Jason. "It makes you uncomfortable when people talk about it."

"Why are you always analyzing my personality?" asked Danya. "Are you a psychologist or something?"

"My mother was one," said Jason. "She taught me a lot about the mind."

"Well, that's your problem then," said Danya. "You're always breaking down how people think and act. Can't you just let people think and act without looking at it like it's a scientific study?"

"I'm just trying to help you," said Jason. "I'm not going to pretend I know exactly what I'm taking about, but you seem like you have no idea who you are right now. Do you know who Na Danya Vih Zalenya is? It seems like you're backing away from everything you said you believed and wanted to do. Why is that?"

"Will you just shut up?" asked Danya. "I don't want to hear your voice right now. I just want to eat my meal in peace."

Jason nodded. "Okay then," he said. "Then I'll go sit at that table."

Jason picked up his tray and brought it over to another vacant table. He began eating his meal again. After a few moments, three other men walked up to the table.

"Excuse me, fine sir," said one of them. He had an odd accent. "Would you mind if we three fighters sit here?"

"No, not at all," said Jason. "My name's Jason. What are your names?"

"I'm Mokar," said Mokar. "And this is Shedi and this is Larki. We never seen your face before. You new to the resistance?"

"I'm new-er," said Jason. "Not new. How about you? I've never seen you before either."

"We're all from Stugora," said Larki. "We're the fightin' Stugorans. We fight to the end and we don't stop."

"You're fightin' to the end, huh?" asked Jason. "Why did you join the resistance?"

"Us three were all Zess farmers," said Shedi. "Every thirty days, Stugora had a holiday to celebrate our independence. Zess was what we'd eat to celebrate. Queen took our holiday and we wouldn't stand for it."

"Why would you celebrate your independence every thirty days?" asked Jason.

"Cause we're Stugorans," said Larki. "We resent that, sir. We're a very proud people, us Stugorans."

"Of course," said Jason. "I never said I had any problem with your people. So you're fighting for Stugoran indepedence again, huh? What did you fight to win independence from the first time?"

"Well, you see, we didn't do any fightin' the first time," said Mokar. "We kindly left the Vazakanian Empire, peacefully."

"You were a part of the Vazakanian Empire?" asked Jason. "How long ago?"

"Long time ago," said Shedi. "We were the eleventh system."

"Why did you decide to leave the Vazakanian Empire?" asked Jason.

"Well, you see," said Mokar, "We just didn't belong with them Vazakanians. They kindly asked us to leave."

"And we told 'em they'd be sorry," said Larki. "You know what we're sayin'?"

"Hold on a second," said Jason. "So, you didn't win independence? The Vazakanian Empire just kicked you out?"

"And we told 'em we were too good for 'em," said Shedi. "They kicked us out and we said good riddance."

"And you celebrate this occasion how many times a year?" asked Jason.

"Fifteen," said Larki. "You got a problem with that? We Stugorans are very proud of our heritage."

"So you celebrate your independence fifteen times a year," said Jason. "You're farmers of some sort of crop that people eat on the holiday. What exactly is it you farm, and why do your people eat it on the holiday?"

"Well, you see," said Mokar, "Zess was what our Darshuk was eatin' when the prime minister told us to scram. Our Darshuk stood up, took the Zess in his hands, and slapped the Vazakanian prime minister across the face with it. He told 'em we weren't good enough for 'em anyway."

"So, what then, is Zess?" asked Jason.

"Lives in lakes and ponds across the planet," said Shedi. "It's a delicacy."

"What animal here on Earth is it like?" asked Jason. "If anything."

"It's like a cuddlefish," said Larki. "That's what they say."

"So, if I understand this," said Jason, "You celebrate the day your leader stood up and slapped the Vazakanian prime minister across the face with a cuddlefish after he kicked you out of the empire. And you celebrate this day fifteen times a year, right? So was the independence a good thing for your planet?"

"Of course," said Mokar. "After the two thousand years of starvation and poverty that followed, we managed to make it on our own just fine."

"I see," said Jason. "Well I hope you get your cuddlefish farms back when we overthrow the Queen."

"Would be good for business," said Larki. "Death to the Vazonian Empire."

"Of course," said Jason. He had finished his meal. "I'll be seeing you three around."

Jason quietly rose from the table and walked away as the three Stugorans ate their meal.

VII: The Queen walked into the hangar and looked at the massive sphere.

[Witness it, your highness,] said Himlen. [The end of the war and the beginning of an era in service of Xiaf.]

[You're sure this device can do what you've told me it can do?] asked the Queen.

[I am certain, your highness,] said Himlen. [This is the Tempest prophesized by Zaxajar.]

[Then let us test it immediately,] said the Queen. [Into the observation craft. We will watch the power of this device.]

Everyone in the hangar filed into the observation craft. The vacuum quickly formed and the craft began towing the device to its destination. The trip through the interstellar medium was short. Once the time dilation drive disengaged, they were in a system crowded with scarred and beaten warships.

[We must place the device in the middle of the fleet,] said Himlen. He piloted the craft toward the center of the formation. [Releasing the device. Pawnsan, set the timer.]

[Setting,] said Pawnsan. [Timer set.]

[Release,] said Himlen. [Weapon armed. Let's get out of here.]

Everyone watched as the timer counted down in Vazakanian numerals while Himlen piloted the observation craft out of the area.

[This distance should be more than safe,] he said. [Everyone, goggles.]

The Queen put the goggles on.

[Fifteen,] said Pawnsan.

The Queen looked out the rear monitor at a heavily cratered moon.

[Seven,] said Pawnsan. [Six. Five. Four. Three. Two. One. Blast, now.]

It was a massive ring of energy: magnificent to view. Even with the goggles, it was blinding. Everyone was forced to turn away.

4:

I: Jason watched as Private First Class Smith went through his training with the other soldiers. It was a sunny morning: there was not a cloud in the sky.

General Ulysses walked up to Jason.

"Constantine," said the General. "This is the final day of training. Is the Union ready to fight?"

"Yes," said Jason. "Watch them. Their execution is flawless."

"Good," said General Ulysses. "We need them to be as ready as possible. We need to make a statement to the Queen that the tide of this war has turned."

"I agree, sir," said Jason. "It's about time we make the Queen play defense."

The General looked around. "Where's the Commander?" he asked. "She working with another unit today?"

"Probably," said Jason. "Can't say for sure."

"Who do you fight for now?" asked the General. "Do you fight for us, or do you fight for them?"

"I fight to restore freedom to the galaxy, sir," said Jason. "That's what I do now. My service with you ended the moment you tried to stop me from defending the planet I swore an oath to protect. I am and will always be an American soldier, sir, but I can no longer offer this country my service. I've outgrown it."

"I should arrest you where you stand for saying that, soldier," said General Ulysses. "I should take you straight to a tribunal and you should be locked away."

"Then do it, sir," said Jason. "Arrest me, right now. But before you do, let me just ask you a question: what plans did you have to rescue me after I crashed on Troyanya? What was the operation called? What was the strategy involved?" Jason shook his head. "Or was a single soldier not worth your time?"

The General was silent.

"And when I managed to make my escape and come home just in time to do what I swore I would do," said Jason, "here you were trying to stop me: you tried to keep me down here on Earth during the battle I'd spent my entire adult life training for." Jason nodded. "So General, let me ask this: do you even deserve my service at this point? Do you deserve me?"

The General was silent for a moment. "Very well, soldier," he said. "Then don't let me get in your way."

The General saluted. Jason returned the salute.

II: Zerpanya stood on the firing range with her weapon. She hit the last target and put her weapon down. The range operator pressed a button and each target moved to the front of the range.

[Every target dead center,] said the operator. [Very fine shooting, Director.]

[I do not miss,] said Zerpanya. [Ever.]

The door to the range slid open and General Yadén walked inside. He held a folder in his hands. [Director,] he said. [Our latest report from the insider has arrived.]

[What does it say, General?] asked Zerpanya.

[We must discuss this privately,] said the General. [It is a very serious matter.]

[Then let us go,] said Zerpanya.

She walked swiftly out of the range, making her way through the facility and into an office. The General kept behind her, closing the door once inside the office.

[The Union and the resistance plan to invade Issius,] said the General. [Immediately. The system is very thinly defended at the moment.]

[We must inform the Queen,] said Zerpanya. [We cannot allow a single system to fall.]

[They intend to use a two wave strategy,] said the General. [The initial wave of warships will take the planet and then the second wave will reinforce the first.]

[I will go to the Queen immediately,] said Zerpanya. [Give me that report. I will discuss it with her.]

III:

The observation craft cruised through the debris field. There was not a single warship left intact.

[I am impressed,] said the Queen. [I have seen all that I need to see. This weapon will go into production immediately. Our goal is now within sight. You will be a hero of the Vazonian Empire, Doctor Himlen.]

[I am most honored by your words, your highness,] said Himlen. [I have only done what you have asked me to do.]

[Let us return to the city,] said the Queen. [I will address the commanders of the military. We will build our new strategy in this war, for Xiaf.]

[For Xiaf,] said Himlen. [May we be blessed.]

Himlen piloted the craft out of the system and engaged the time dilation drive. The journey was, again, short. The craft landed on the royal landing pad and the Queen left the vessel, returning to the palace. She hit the button on the arm of the throne and Kedán walked into the room.

[Yes, your highness?] he asked.

[Kedán,] said the Queen. [Call an assembly of military command. I have much to discuss with them.]

[At once, your highness,] said Kedán. He hurried out of the room.

IV: "Never," screamed Danya. She opened her eyes and looked around as she awoke. Everyone in the cabin of the transport was now looking at her.

"What?" she yelled. "What are you looking at? I could kill all of you."

Everyone looked away. The transport landed inside the Shadow Base. After a few moments, the ramp lowered and Danya was the first one to exit the vessel. She went to her room and locked herself inside.

V: Jason sighed as he made his way through the base. He walked up to the door of Grand General Sazún's quarters, knocking on it. After a moment, the door opened.

"Jason," said Sazún. "Is there a problem?"

"Commander Danya is in no condition to fight, sir," he said. "I'm beginning to fear that she may try to hurt herself again or hurt others this time."

"Why do you say this?" asked Sazún. "What behavior have you seen in her?"

"She's become very unstable, sir," said Jason. "After she met General Ulysses, she just seemed different. She isolated herself from everyone while we were there. And on the flight back over here, she woke up from sleeping, screamed the word, 'never,' and then yelled at everyone for staring at her. She told us that she could kill all of us."

"She said she could kill all of you?" asked Sazún. "What was her tone?"

"She was angry, sir," said Jason. "I have no idea what could be happening in her mind right now, but I don't think she should be allowed into battle right now."

"I will have a psychologist talk to her," said Sazún. "I thought she had finally found peace with her past. What more could there be to tell?"

"I have no idea, sir," said Jason. "But something still isn't right."

"Where is the Commander now?" asked Sazún. "Do you know?"

"Probably in her quarters," said Jason. "I don't know for sure."

"Then thank you for bringing this to my attention," said Sazún. "I will handle this matter. If you'll excuse me now, I have many things to do at the moment."

"Of course, sir," said Jason. He left the office and made his way to the common room. He found the usual Vazakanian crowd at their usual table. They all looked up at him.

"Something wrong?" asked Jason.

"Why do you ask?" asked Sabenya.

"All right," said Jason. "What have you heard?"

"What have we heard?" asked Sabenya. "What do you mean?"

"Someone must have said something to you," he said. "There were twenty-five people on the transport and they all saw the same thing."

"We have no idea what you're talking about," said Sabenya.

"We? Can you read minds?" asked Jason. "How do you know everyone at this table has no idea what I'm talking about?"

Everyone was silent.

"For the sake of her well-being," said Jason. "Don't spread rumors about her. Danya just needs time to figure herself out."

"A Vazakanian never spreads rumors," said Sabenya. "It's forbidden in our culture."

"Which is probably why we can't resist rumors when we hear them," said Tofán. "Vazakanians love to hear details."

Jason shook his head. "Why doesn't that surprise me?" he asked. "Just curious: how do any of you take each other seriously?"

"We don't," said Sabenya. "Not unless we have to. It's the Vazakanian Lifestyle. When we take things seriously, that means there's a problem. Otherwise, we find it's best to be as ridiculous as possible. Laughter keeps us in good spirits. Think about it."

Jason was silent as he thought.

"We're not honestly as ridiculous as you think we are at heart," said Sabenya. "Vazakanians really are deep thinkers, but only when we need to be. You know how we feel about balance: it's all about having a balanced mind. That's all the Vazakanian Way is. We know the lifestyle Vazakanians choose to live while following the Vazakanian Way can be distracting to others; you know, with the sexual perversion and all, but we know what we're doing and that's all that matters."

"So what you're saying," said Jason, "is that you're actually trying to be ridiculous so you're not always on edge and feeling stress?"

"Yes," said Sabenya. "That's how Vazakanians like to live. We like to laugh at ourselves. It's almost competitive in a way: as long as it's all in good fun, anything goes, really."

"But how do you have any sense of what's all in good fun and what's not then?" asked Jason.

"That's where the Vazakanian Way takes effect," said Sabenya. "It's all about balance. We balance our thoughts with our instincts. We think things out carefully and we trust our instincts. It's not foolproof. Every now and then, we'll make a bad decision, but for the most part, that's what makes a Vazakanian."

Jason was silent. He nodded. "I think I understand," he said. "I think I get it now. Your lifestyle isn't the Vazakanian Way. The Vazakanian Way is just the philosophy that allows you to have a balanced mind while you live your lifestyle."

"Exactly," said Sabenya. "The Vazakanian lifestyle just happens to be our lifestyle of choice. The Vazakanian Way could work with many different lifestyles."

"What lifestyles couldn't it work with?" asked Jason.

"Ones that don't allow you to control your own life or make your own decisions," said Sabenya. "It's just a philosophy."

"So why did the Queen persecute people for following it?" asked Jason.

"Because if people trusted the Vazakanian Way, then there would be no reason to blindly follow a government, or a religion, or a movement, or a corporation, or even another lifestyle that already had all of the answers to your life's challenges predetermined," said Sabenya. "That's what Xiaf is: it's not just a religion. It's the easy way out of being responsible for your own life. Xiaf could have been anything during the dark time at the end of the Vazakanian Empire. It could have been a different religion, a new political party, a different philosophy even. The point is that it could have been anything that claimed to have all the answers already determined for us. But it just so happened that the easy way out was to follow a businesswoman turned tyrant who claimed to be a prophet. You can go across time and culture and find the same story everywhere. I'm sure it must have happened at some point right here on Earth."

"How do you know all of this?" asked Jason. "I thought you couldn't read or write."

"Danya told me to say that as part of your training," said Sabenya. "I'm a survivor of the house of Moradonya."

"What does that mean?" asked Jason.

"It means she's smarter than you are or can ever hope to be," said Tofán. "She comes from the family that founded the empire's first and proudest university. She'd better be smart. She has a legacy to uphold once we win this war. Her family was a bunch of freaks, but they sure knew what they were talking about when it came to philosophy."

"Did you ever worship Xiaf?" asked Jason.

"I did for a while," said Sabenya. "Or I pretended to, at least. I sang in the choir at a Temple of Xiaf and then when I turned about fifteen, I decided to marry a man that often prayed there as his sex slave."

"Why did you decide to do that?" asked Jason.

"Because I already knew who he was," said Sabenya. "He was an instructor at the university. He taught me everything I know."

"About using your body or about the Vazakanian Way?" asked Tofán. "Because you have very good knowledge of both. Just ask any of the men or women at this table."

"I learned everything from him," said Sabenya. "Everything. And when he was arrested for doing that, Grand General Sazún convinced the Queen that he could teach me to follow Xiaf again. He took me in, and after about a year, he, Danya, and I defected to the resistance."

"And ever since," said Tofán, "She's taken it upon herself to keep the men and women of the resistance satisfied wherever she goes."

"Well, the way I see it, someone around here has to be a Vazakanian," said Sabenya. "I don't want us to forget what we are." She paused. "And the way I do that just happens to be very sexual. If you want, I'll show you what I'm talking about. I promise you that I can take your mind off of Danya for a while."

"Are you kidding me?" asked Jason. "That's the most disturbing concept I've ever heard out of a girl's mouth. You just volunteered to substitue your body for hers."

"It's a common practice in Vazakanian culture," said Sabenya. "And Danya is Vazakanian, remember. She'll understand."

"Sorry," said Jason. "I'm in love with her. I don't think I could do that."

"You're in love with her?" asked Sabenya. "How can you be in love with her if you don't know who she really is?"

"I couldn't tell you," said Jason. "Sometimes love just doesn't make sense."

"Very true," said Sabenya. "A lot of people are obsessed with finding reasons for love. But sometimes, it just happens." She paused. "I have an extra bed in my room. You can sleep in it if you don't want to share one with me. The offer stands though."

"He obviously doesn't understand what he's refusing," said Tofán. "From one man to another, you should really take the offer."

"Why?" asked Jason.

"If you want to love Danya, then you can't simply ignore her culture," said Sabenya. "She'll have to accept parts of yours, and you'll have to accept parts of hers. Vazakanians do not make commitments with lust. We only make commitments with love. We believe strongly in sexual freedom, well, within reason. It helps to be rational on this matter, but we believe that sexual monogamy is an irrational concept: it's unhealthy."

"I'm sorry," said Jason. "It doesn't feel right to do that."

5:

I: [The device is called the Tempest,] said the Queen. [And we will use it at Issius. We will launch it at the incoming enemy fleet and we will watch as it destroys them all. They will never know what hit them.]

[Your highness,] said Zerpanya. [Perhaps we should look into our strategy further. I believe that any strategy must be fully thought out before it is used.]

[What more could we do with the strategy, Director?] asked the Queen. [The power of the weapon will speak for itself. It will be a great storm of Xiaf to finally purge the galaxy of filth.]

[Yes, your highness,] said Zerpanya. [But to say that we simply launch it at the fleet and run: well, isn't that somewhat simplistic?]

[That is all we need to do, Director,] said the Queen. [We will keep the planet thinly defended so as to make them believe we know nothing of the attack. And then when the time comes, we will launch the weapon. It will crush them.]

[Yes, your highness,] said Zerpanya.

II: General Ulysses looked out over the base as night fell over the East Coast of the country. All was dark.

A light went on in the distance. General Ulysses looked at it for a moment. It flickered and flashed, almost as if in code.

Ulysses left the tower, heading outside. He walked across the base toward the light. He came to a field just beyond the landing pad. He drew closer and closer to the light.

It was Private First Class Joe Smith.

"Smith," said General Ulysses. "What are you doing out here? The big day is tomorrow."

Smith took a look at the General and immediately made a run toward the spacecraft parked on the landing pad.

"Smith," yelled General Ulysses. "Get back here. What are you doing?"

Ulysses looked over at the light. He reached into his pocket, feeling the pistol he'd confiscated from Commander Danya. He drew it and pointed it at Smith.

"Freeze, Private," said General Ulysses. "Or I'll shoot."

Smith stopped. He had just made it onto the landing pad. General Ulysses kept the weapon pointed at Smith as Ulysses stepped toward him.

"Walk, private," said Ulysses. "Hands up, to the station. Let's go: on the double."

Ulysses watched as Smith put his hands up and walked toward the base. General Ulysses followed him with the pistol. The General came to an alarm. Ulysses punched it. The alarm sounded and a number of armed guards quickly made their way to the scene.

"Arrest him," said Ulysses. "He's a spy."

"Due process," said Smith. "It's in the constitution."

"You're in the military," said Ulysses. "You're an enemy combatant. There is no due process in the military for this very reason: on the eve of a massive military campaign that could determine the fate of an entire nation, we find a spy among us. This is what the law is designed for. You will go before a tribunal immediately."

One of the guards walked up to Smith to cuff him.

"Disarm yourself, officer," said Ulysses. "Ven Thar combat move: he'll grab you and take your weapon."

The MP officer disarmed himself and approached Smith with only the pair of handcuffs. The other guards had their weapons carefully trained on the spy.

Ulysses held his breath. The Officer cuffed Smith without a problem.

"Bring him to interrogation," said General Ulysses. "Immediately."

"Yes, sir," said the officer in command.

III: Jason followed Sabenya into her room. She turned the light on and pointed to the bed against the left wall.

"You can sleep there," she said. "This will be pretty neat for me. I haven't slept alone in a bed since I was fifteen years old."

"Are you proud of that?" asked Jason.

"Very," said Sabenya. She pulled her sash loose and removed both her top and her skirt in one quick motion as if she weren't even aware of what she was doing. Jason stared at the sight. She quickly kicked her boots off as she sat down on the side of her bed and leaned back, widening her stance as most she could. She looked down at herself there. "I don't even remember most of them," she said. "In all honesty. Every Vazakanian girl will tell you something like that because she'll want to impress you, but the truth is that most Vazakanian women aren't even close to as wildly promiscuous as they claim to be. You just have to understand our culture: that's a desirable quality in a woman. So it's just a matter of pride for us when we embellish the truth. But in my case, at least, I guess you could say that men in the resistance wouldn't know what to do with themselves if I weren't there for them. It's almost become my role in the resistance now. No one realizes I can actually fight and no one realizes I'm actually very smart." She shrugged her shoulders. "But I wouldn't have it any other way," she said. "Vazakanians love to be ridiculous."

"You don't say?" asked Jason. He had hardly heard her words. He stared at the finely shaped rill of the loose bound enchantment wrinkled forth from within about the gentle seam of a comforting rift running vertically to a smooth fleshy cusp from above. It was beautiful. His mind raced with the many possibilities it presented. Sabenya nodded.

"Do you understand what you are to Vazakanian women?" she asked. "You're what we dream of." She closed her stance where she sat. Jason leveled his gaze with hers.

"How am I what you dream of?" asked Jason.

"Just the fact you'd ask that question proves my point," said Sabenya. "You're a sexually liberated man. On one hand, you have the sensitivity and control to stand in front of a naked woman and speak calmly and respectfully like it makes no difference to you, no matter how excited you are. And then, on the other hand, you have no problem letting the fullest of your libido show when it's appropriate. I've heard about what you do to Danya. Vazakanian men could learn a lot from you. You embrace your libido, but you're in control of it." Sabenya nodded her head. "How attractive do you find me?" she asked. "Be honest. I'd really like to know what you think."

Jason stood up and stepped up to her. She stood up as well before him, looking him in the eyes, her sapphire gaze meeting his own.

"You're very unique," said Jason. "Distinctive. You're a break from all the blonde hair and green eyes. You stand out."

They stared at each other in silence for a moment. Neither said anything. Jason looked down at her body from where he stood, silent as she smiled. Jason shook his head.

"And you're so, so fine," he said.

Jason wrapped his left arm around her and kissed her, reaching back with his right hand behind her and grabbing her rear as he did so. He stroked her there for a moment and then slapped her there as he continued to kiss her, but then he leaned down and drew his tongue gently across the hanging drifts of her breasts, sucking on them and kissing them with his hands held tenderly on her hips. Sabenya beamed with pride as he did so. She pulled back and smiled.

"So, what would you like to do tonight?" she asked. "I'll do anything you want, and I mean anything."

"Anything?" asked Jason. "I'm going to hold you to that."

"I will do things no man could ever imagine," said Sabenya. "Things Danya can't do, and things no other

185

woman in the galaxy can do. I know what your favorite thing to do to Danya is. I usually have to beg Vazakanian and even non-Vazakanian men for that." She held her mouth to his ear and whispered. "I want to feel your knuckles," she said. "Your thumb too. I want them all coaxing that one spot every girl craves to have coaxed. You have no idea how exciting it is for a Vazakanian girl to see that kind of primal and raw perversion in a man. You have no idea." She reached her right hand down into his pants and grabbed his now-hardened length. "Take control of me," she whispered. "Let that liberated mind of yours run wild. I want to see what you can do to a girl."

IV:

Jason kissed Sabenya again and again as he worked himself in and out of her flesh for the sixth time of the night. He held her breasts in his hands as she groaned. Her flesh was soft, so soft, so, so soft. It was smooth and wet and warm: it was heavenly, much like Danya's flesh: the most comforting thing he'd ever felt in his life. It was like a dream. Sabenya groaned as she felt her pleasure again. It was too much for him. He pulled out of her and knelt over her chest as he exhaled and released over her breasts again. His pleasure flowed forth in pulse after pulse as her own wet warmth flooded out of her flesh behind him. He emptied his passion onto her breasts as she looked up at him with a smile. He shook his head. The feeling was so intense, more so than it had been all night. It pulsed and pulsed and pulsed with more and more of his warm delight, completely covering her breasts and beginning to drip off of them. It seemed endless.

"Is that all you've got?" asked Sabenya. "I'm disappointed. I wanted to go swimming."

"Shut up, you slut," said Jason. "I never said you could talk."

"I'm sorry," said Sabenya. "I was just expecting more."

"When will you learn?" asked Jason. "You're a slut and you don't have any right to talk unless I give you permission. I'm going to have to fuck those perfect slight-sagging tits now."

Jason sat on her chest and submerged his length between her breasts, beginning to work it back and forth between them as he held them tight against it with his hands. He closed his eyes and savored the feeling of her flowing curves, so warm and slick with his own passion against his hardened push. They were so large and round around him: soft, fleshy: they were a drifting cloud of a nurturing paradise. It was too intense. He could take no more.

He released again. She pushed forth her tongue to collect his warmth and savor the taste as it pulsed forth from within. He covered her breasts further, and then her face, filling her tongue to her joyful delight. He continued to coax his length with his own hand for a moment more as his pleasure began to die away. He exhaled and closed his eyes slowly as the final heavenly pulse came and went. He rolled off next to her and watched as she began licking her breasts clean in the way he'd instructed her to do.

"Look at you," said Jason. "Licking it off your own tits. Admit it. Admit you're a filthy slut."

Sabenya smiled. "The most notorious one in the galaxy," she said. "I told you I'm good. Any time you want a break from Danya, just come to me and I'll give you something different. I'll always take care of you. I'll do anything. Well, I'll do anything but love you. Romantically, I prefer women, to be honest. But I'm happy to lend my body to a man in need anytime."

"I'm curious though," said Jason. "Why are you happy to do this if you prefer women?"

"Only romantically," said Sabenya. "You have to understand how a Vazakanian looks at sex. For me, at least, sexuality is the most unique and special element of human nature. It fascinates me and I love to explore it in every way possible."

"But why in this way?" asked Jason. "If you're romantically attracted to women, why would you ever want to have sex with men that just want to objectify you and degrade you and pretend you're someone else? I thought you were a feminist."

"You really want me to answer that, or would you like to just go on with the completely naïve mentality you have about women and sex?" asked Sabenya.

"Well, Danya did warn me about getting a lecture from you," said Jason. "I suppose I should hear it."

"I'll cut to the chase then," said Sabenya. "What you think you see in the person I am is your own culture's problem: you take exception to a woman who chooses to live the way I do, as if a woman can't do it and be empowered. You blindly find it hard to take a promiscuous woman seriously no matter what more there is to her as a person. So, let me ask you something: what if I told you that, in my culture, it's okay for women to love sex? In fact, it's encouraged. Women in my culture take pride in their sexuality. We empower ourselves through it. Women in your culture could learn a thing or two from women in my culture. Sure, Vazakanian woman may be genetically modified to the point where we have no consequences to worry about: we're immune to just about all forms of disease, we only bleed once every four years, and we've been specifically modified to be as attractive as possible to men, even to the point where our bodies do things like ejaculate when we feel pleasure, but your women could certainly stop being afraid of sexual desire. Men want to fuck women. And that will never change. How they want to do that might change like it has in my culture, but the fact of the matter is that women will never achieve equality unless they accept that men want to fuck women and they learn to deal with it. I don't understand why they're disgusted when it's apparent that a man wants nothing but sex from them. Lust is not disgusting. The perception that love must come before sex is a product of a patriarchical society. It stems from a man's desire to possess a woman solely for himself. Do you know what Vazakanian women did over seventy-five hundred years ago? We stopped trying to change the basic nature of men. Instead, we sexually liberated ourselves. We stopped fearing lust. In time, we learned that it could be beautiful when men lust for us. We learned to embrace it. We learned to confront the problem instead of shying away from it. It turned out that if women wanted equality, then they had to change themselves. The same is the case for all matters of social equality. You can't solve a problem that comes from living in a patriarchy with a patriarchical mentality. So now that I've told you all of this, why wouldn't a woman be allowed to be a slut and be proud of it? Why should that idea be so bizarre?"

Jason was silent.

"What do you think?" asked Sabenya. "Why shouldn't a woman be allowed to be a student of human sexuality? That's what I am. Human sexuality fascinates me intellectually. I understand it better than just about everyone else in the galaxy. And, of course, I enjoy indulging in the pleasure it gives me. Why shouldn't a woman be allowed to look at sex the way I do?"

"You should be allowed to," said Jason. "I didn't realize you had this all thought out."

"You thought I had no control over my own libido?" asked Sabenya. "You thought I was just blindly surrendering to my desires every time I have sex. Fuck no. I know exactly what I'm doing. I go out of my way to be as seductive and flirtatious as possible in the presence of men. I do it because I enjoy seeing that look in their eyes: the lust for me. It empowers me. That's a matriarchical type of empowerment."

"Well, as long as you're proud of it," said Jason. "This definitely takes my mind off of Danya. I won't lie. And that's what you promised me after all."

"I know," said Sabenya. The tone of her voice changed. She smiled. "I'm very good at this."

"I just hope she gets through this whole mess," said Jason. "I really hope she does."

"What do you think could be wrong with her?" asked Sabenya. "I thought she'd let everything out."

"Me too," said Jason. "I have no idea." He paused. "It all started with General Ulysses. When she met him, she changed."

"What did he say to her?" asked Sabenya.

"First, he confiscated her pistol," said Jason. "And she told him that he had a very narrow-minded view of what a weapon was. And then he told her that far more people could use a gun as a weapon than whatever else she was trained to use."

"Did he ever give the gun back?" asked Sabenya.

Jason paused. "No," he said. "Maybe that's it. Maybe it has something to do with the gun. But I've seen Danya without it before. She doesn't always have it with her."

"Then what else could it be?" asked Sabenya.

"I don't know," said Jason. "I'm just very worried about her."

V:
Danya opened her eyes, shaking her head in horror.

"What are you thinking about right now?" asked the doctor.

"Winning this war," said Danya. "Destroying the Vazakanian Empire, I mean the Vazonian Empire."

"Which do you mean?" asked the doctor. "Do you mean the Vazakanian Empire or the Vazonian Empire?"

"Seriously," said Danya. "Do you think I don't know what empire I'm trying to destroy?"

"What do you think?" asked the doctor. "This is about you."

"I'll tell you what I think," said Danya. "I think you should clear me to do what I've trained to do since I was seventeen years old."

"And what is that?" asked the doctor.

"Destroy the Vazonian Empire," said Danya. "To think that I need your permission to join the battle is disgraceful."

"What did you do before you were seventeen years old?" asked the doctor.

"I was a sex slave," said Danya. "Which was a lot more fun than this."

"A lot more fun than what?" asked the Doctor.

"This," said Danya. "Sitting here in interrogation because I said something I didn't mean. We all say things we don't mean. I'm sure you say things you don't mean all the time. Don't you?"

"Of course," said the doctor. "But, Danya, the people around you have all noticed a change in you."

"What people around me?" asked Danya. "I don't talk to anyone."

"You don't?" asked the doctor. "Do you have any friends?"

"No," said Danya. "I don't like to get too close to people that might die tomorrow."

"I see," said the doctor. "You don't believe its worth your time to build relationships with people simply because they might die."

"In wartime," said Danya. "Once all this ends, I can see myself making a lot of friends."

"Really?" asked the doctor. "What kinds of friends will you make?"

"I don't know," said Danya. "Why does it matter? We live here in the present. That future is very far away."

"A moment ago, you seemed excited to discuss it," said the doctor. "Why the change?"

"Can I leave now?" asked Danya. "There's a battle I have to prepare for."

"I can't clear you to go participate in this battle," said the Doctor. "You're not ready."

"I'm not ready?" asked Danya. "Then how much longer until I'm ready?"

"You tell me," said the doctor. "How much longer until you're ready?"

"How the fuck would I know?" asked Danya. "You're the fucking doctor. Tell me what I need to tell you."

"Why don't you stop yelling, Danya, and tell me what you need to tell me instead?" asked the doctor. "Tell me. What is it?"

"Fuck this," said Danya. "I'm going to the Air Force Base and no one here is going to stop me."

She rose from the chair and left the room, walking through the base to the hangar. There were no spacecraft in it.

Danya cried out as loudly as she could and picked up a cone, throwing at the wall.

VI: "I'm afraid the Queen may know we're coming," said General Ulysses. "I found a spy at the training base."

"This is not good," said Sazún. "The element of surprise was vital to this operation. I assume that the Queen has reinforced Issius now?"

"She has not," said General Ulysses. "Almost as if, well, as if she wants us to invade."

"If that is what she wants," said Sazún. "Then we cannot give it to her. My senses would tell me we'd be walking into a trap."

"I concur, Grand General," said General Ulysses. "Which is why I propose that we alter our strategy."

"What do you propose, General?" asked Sazún.

"That we launch this operation backwards," said General Ulysses. "We get our troops on the ground to win the planet and we set up a blockade around the perimeter of the planet and its moon to ensure that the Queen can't reinforce her own troops. We will win the battle with the people on the ground."

"This could catch the Queen off-guard," said Sazún. "We will do it."

"Our warships will arrive in small waves," said General Ulysses. "Perhaps twenty per wave."

"We will launch at midnight," said Sazún. "Let the battle begin."

VII: Director Zerpanya rushed into the royal chamber and knelt before the Queen.

[Your highness,] said Zerpanya. [One of our spies has been discovered. The Union and the resistance may know Issius is a trap.]

[Nothing can stop the power of the Tempest,] said the Queen. [The strategy remains as planned. The Tempest will destroy the filth.]

[Your highness,] said Zerpanya. [We've thought more deeply about the utilization of this weapon and we can see several scenarios which will render it ineffective.]

[Impossible,] said the Queen. [I have witnessed the power of this weapon myself. Nothing can stop it. It is the Tempest prophesized by Zaxajar.]

[Your highness,] said Zerpanya. [It is simply a weapon developed by scientists. If we do not change our strategy, then we could lose this battle.]

[It goes as planned,] said the Queen. [There will be no more discussion of this.]

6:

I: There was a knock on the door. The room fell silent. The door burst open. Four heavily armed officers stood at the door.

[Ven Thar,] said the officer at the head of the formation. [You're all under arrest.]

[And what are the charges against us?] asked the bartender.

[Suspicion of crimes against Xiaf,] said the soldier. [The warrant comes straight from the Queen herself.]

All the men and women in the bar stood up.

[If those are the charges,] said one of the men, [then you can take your warrant and you can shove it up your ass.]

[We've grown tired of the Queen and her god,] said one of the women in the bar. [We say that it is time for the Queen to leave this planet and never come back.]

[Really?] asked the soldier. [And what gives you the right to say that?]

One of the men in the bar reached beneath a table and pulled out a heavy machine gun. [This,] he said. He opened fire on the officers, killing all four of them.

Every man and woman in the bar walked over to the dead officers and started dragging them out the door. A woman ran up to the bell in the square and began ringing it.

[Let the revolution begin,] she yelled. [Death to the Vazonian Empire.]

II: Jason disengaged the time dilation drive.

"All units report," he said.

Each shadow unit confirmed its presence.

"Form perimeter and launch personnel carriers," said Jason. "Make this quick."

The wave of warships joined the rest of the perimeter as the troop transports made their way to Issius.

"Enemies incoming," said Sabenya.

"Engage," said Jason.

The sound of the rail guns filled the cabin.

"Look at that enemy carrier over there," said Jason. "They seem to be shielding it for some reason."

"They're in a defensive formation around it," said Sabenya.

"All units, attack the enemy carrier," said Jason. "Let's not find out why they're protecting it."

III: The Vazonian commander stood on board the carrier watching the advancing wave of enemy assault ships.

[Fire, fire,] he yelled. [Don't let them get through.]

[They're too close, sir,] yelled another officer.

[Launch the package,] said the Commander. [Do it.]

[Launching Tempest,] said the officer. [In three, two, one, launch.]

IV: Jason watched as a large sphere launched from the enemy carrier.

"What the hell is that?" asked Jason.

"I don't know," said Sabenya. "All units, target and destroy unknown object."

"No," said Jason. "Target with EMP pulse only. Disable unknown object and capture it."

"Why?" asked Sabenya.

"I have a gut feeling," said Jason. "That this is why it's too easy."

"Allied Command to Shadow One," said Sazún. "What does this object look like?"

"Like a ball covered will smaller ball bearings," said Jason. "We're in the process of capturing it now."

V: The city streets echoed with the sound of gunfire. A squadron of Vazonian guards ran for cover as the civilians threw Molotov cocktails in their direction. From the sky, Union personnel transports and gunships could be seen all around giving support to the battle.

The citizens of the capital stood before the gates of the capital building chanting.

[Kolanto su no podavento, kolanto su no podavento, kolanto su no podavento,] they yelled.

A man lit a pipe bomb and threw it through the window of the building. It exploded.

The people broke through the gates and tore down the door to the building. The guards inside opened fire on them, but there were too many people. They came to the governor's office. They pushed as hard as they could. Two men picked up a statue of Xiaf and threw it at the door. The door split in two. The people pried the door open. The guards inside the office threw tear gas into the crowd, but it had no effect.

The governor was dragged out of the building and brought into the city squre. The people threw rocks and sticks and garbage at him.

[You will all be put to death,] said the governor. [You are all traitors to Xiaf and to the Vazonian Empire.]

[Hang him,] said one of the women in the crowd. [Hang him high.]

VI: Zerpanya burst through the doors of the royal chamber.

[The worst has happened, your highness,] said Zerpanya. [Issius is lost.]

[What nonsense do you speak of?] asked the Queen.

[The weapon could not be used effectively,] said Zerpanya. [It failed.]

The Queen stood up. [How could it have failed?] she asked. [It is the Tempest.]

[The Union simply disabled it and towed it away,] said Zerpanya. [And down on the planet itself, the citizens have taken to the streets to help the Union and the resistance fight. I'd recommend falling back while we still can.]

[Never,] said the Queen. [We will fight to the death. Send in reinforcements.]

[Impossible,] said Zerpanya. [The Union and the resistance have formed a blockade around the planet.]

[Then let us pray to Xiaf that our men on the ground may find the strength to overcome,] said the Queen. [Let us pray.]

[Prayer will not give us reinforcements,] said Zerpanya. [We must retreat.]

[To the death,] said the Queen. [Always to the death. That is what Xiaf commands of us.]

VII:
Dead Vazonian guards lined the streets as the liberation force marched on with the flag of Issius. As they marched on, the people in the buildings above opened their widows and cheered the liberation force on. Across the surface of the planet, the scene was much the same: entire legions of Vazonian soldiers marched with their hands on their heads in a show of surrender down the rural and suburban streets of the planet. And the people were celebrating. The Union and the resistance had very quickly taken the planet.

VIII:
"All units, report," said Jason.

"Ground force one," said the communicator. "We have taken the capital city. The governor has been executed."

Jason listened as each report followed the same premise.

"Allied Command to Shadow One," said Sazún. "Preliminary mission complete. We must now stabilize the planet and spread the news across the galaxy: it is time, time to stand up and fight."

IX: *"Come, young one," said the masked woman. "It is time for another sacrifice. This time you will perform the ritual yourself."*

The child followed the masked woman through the palace to the chamber. Another man lay chained to the altar. The child gazed into the ruby eyes of the altar. The woman removed her mask to reveal the younger face of Queen Jonarka.

[I am your servant,] said the child. Her voice was feminine. [Keep my spirit pure as I offer to you a sacrifice of rotted faith.]

The girl bowed and stepped forward, removing the sacrificial sword from its sheath.

[I offer to Xiaf a sacrifice of a rotted soul,] said the young girl. [To keep me pure as I do what is bidden of me in your name.]

The girl approached the helpless man, lifting the sword high over her head and looking down at the man, into his eyes, seeing the fear within them. The young girl brought the sword down as hard as she could. The young girl took her mask off. The face of a young Princess Danya lay beneath it.

[Excellent, Danya,] said the Queen. [You are ready to lead an Empire in the name of Xiaf.]

Danya screamed as loudly as she could and punched the punching bag. It was now beaten full of holes.

"I didn't do it," she screamed. "I never did it."

She reached to her holster. Her pistol wasn't there. She reached deeper into her holster. The weapon still wasn't there. She spun around and kicked the punching bag as hard as she could, breaking it open. The stuffing poured out onto the floor. Danya collapsed to her knees and buried her face in her hands. She pulled her hands away and cried out again.

"I never did it," she yelled. "Never. I'm not evil."

"Enough, Danya," said General Hatshenya.

Danya turned to look at the General. Ex-General Kufán Vih Sensán stood next to her.

"I'm told you actually have met General Kufán before," said Hatshenya. "On the night we tried to assassinate the Queen. I think I understand now the struggle within your mind. You conducted the sacrifice as a child, didn't you, Danya? The Queen was training you to become her successor."

Danya closed her eyes and shook her head. "No," she said. "I'm not evil."

"You were a child," said Kufán. "Brainwashed into thinking death was essential to your well-being. When I saw you that night, I did not see a monster. I saw a helpless child who knew no better than simply doing what she was told to do. It was not a conscious decision."

Tears fell from Danya's eyes to the rock floor. She shook her head.

"I'm not evil," she said. She shook her head again. "Never."

"What did I tell you to remember?" asked Hatshenya. "Don't go blaming yourself for a conflict vastly greater than yourself. You are not evil. As a child, your innocence was exploited. Live with it. Be at peace with it. Balance is the Vazakanian Way."

Danya was silent for a moment. She shook her head once more. "Never," she said. "I'm not evil."

"No one will believe you are," said Hatshenya. "They will understand the life you've been forced to live. Perhaps some will not, but there will always be some who simply never will understand, with all issues of conscience. Be at peace, Danya. Be at peace. Accept it: your innocence was exploited and there was nothing you could do. Do you hear me? There was nothing you could do. There was nothing you could do. Say it: there was nothing you could do."

Danya was silent. She looked away from Kufán and Hatshenya, looking instead into the darkness of the room.

"Say it, Danya," said Hatshenya. "There was nothing you could do."

Danya was silent.

"Say it," said Hatshenya. "There was nothing you could do."

Danya took a deep breath. She opened her mouth to speak but then closed it.

"Say it," said Hatshenya. "Speak it from your heart."

Danya turned and looked into the light where Hatshenya and Kufán stood. "There was" she paused. "There was nothing I could do," she said.

"Believe it," said Hatshenya. "There was nothing you could do."

Danya repeated herself. "There was nothing I could do," she said.

"Do you believe it, Danya?" asked Hatshenya. "Do you believe there was nothing you could do?"

"There was nothing I could do," said Danya. She shook her head. "Nothing I could do."

"Yes," said Hatshenya. "Say it like you mean it. Be brave."

Danya took a deep breath and looked up at Hatshenya. "There was nothing I could have done," she said. "Because I was just a child."

X: Jason landed the assault ship in the hangar of the Shadow Base. He jumped down out of the craft as quickly as he could. Many others had already arrived at the base. They were all ecstatic as each craft landed.

Jason stepped out of his flight suit. Sabenya did the same behind him. She then wrapped her arms around him and kissed him.

"You've made yourself a hero to the entire galaxy," she said. "You're a great pilot."

Jason smirked. "And you're the deadliest slut I've ever met in my life," he said. He reached behind her with his right hand and slid it beneath her skirt. He grabbed her rear and began stroking it. He spoke softly. "Victory sex?" he asked. "Here in front of everyone?"

Danya walked up to the two of them. It was clear by the look of her eyes that she had been crying. Sabenya and Jason let go of each other. Danya said nothing for a moment.

"Do you two love each other?" she asked. "Is that what I'm seeing?"

"No, Danya," said Sabenya, "He has no feelings for me. I'd never do that to you. I just wanted to lighten his attitude a little. He was worrying about you too much. It wasn't healthy." She nodded. "I'll leave you two to talk. Don't let me get in your way."

She walked away. Jason watched as she stepped up to the three Stugorans and began smiling at them and charming them as if she'd forgotten about him entirely.

"You don't love her?" asked Danya. "Be honest."

"She obviously isn't capable of loving men," said Jason. "She and I are just friends."

"How do you know?" asked Danya. "How do you know you have no feelings for her?"

"There's only one thing I can ever imagine doing with her," said Jason. "And it's not just sitting and talking. Trust me."

Danya looked over at Sabenya. Her back was turned to the two of them as she let her top fall to the floor behind her, leaving her torso bare, much to the delight of the crowd of men around her.

"It's just a game to her," said Jason. "She doesn't take it the least bit seriously with men. She just likes the feeling of having power over a man's desire."

"I guess you're right," said Danya. She stepped up to Jason and hugged him. She kissed him. "I'm sorry about my behavior lately," she said. "It's just that I was afraid you'd think I was evil if you knew the truth about me."

"What is the truth about you?" asked Jason.

"Jason," said Danya, "I was not ignorant to what my mother was doing while I was growing up. She'd educated me about faith in Xiaf, she'd trained me to command the military, and to spread propaganda, and I even conducted human sacrifices, not because I wanted to, but because she'd convinced me I had to if I wanted to survive. She exploited my innocence and there was nothing I could do."

"I'd suspected something like that," said Jason. "But what suddenly brought that part of your past to the front of your mind?"

"The mention of swords," said Danya. "The sacrifice is conducted with a sword."

Jason nodded. "Now it all makes sense," he said. "Have you found peace with that part of your life?"

"I find peace in the fact that I'm now working to make it right," said Danya. "I'm now doing the right thing."

"So why did you really run away?" asked Jason. "What made you decide to leave her?"

"I didn't lie about that," said Danya. "The servant in the palace gave his life to make me realize the evil I was involved with."

Jason nodded. "So, Danya," he said. "Do you love me?"

"You were the only one to ever be concerned about the person I was," said Danya. "You saw something in me that just didn't seem right and you cared about me. Yes, Jason, I love you." She paused. "Do you love me?"

"You're the only thing I can think about when I'm not fighting," said Jason. "I love you and I'm overjoyed to see that you've found peace with yourself."

Danya kissed Jason. "You still up for that victory sex?" she asked. "I can give a man good victory sex too. Sabenya isn't the only girl who can give sex with a theme to it."

"Before we get too excited," said Jason, "General Ulysses told me this belonged to you."

Jason handed Danya her pistol. She holstered it.

7:

I: General Ulysses stood at the podium before the Interstellar Council.

"News of the Vazonian defeat at Issius has spread rapidly across the galaxy over the past weeks," he said. "Fueled by the resistance, the anti-Vazonian sentiment across the galaxy has never been stronger. Rebel militias are springing up all across the empire. It is my belief that if we could support these efforts, then we can march on the royal palace on precisely the day that the Vazonian Empire was formed. People of the Interstellar Union, the demise of the empire is near. At this very moment, the Queen is forced to use her military to silence her own people. It is the perfect time to sweep across the galaxy and take this war directly to the heart of the empire. I make a motion to go on a campaign straight for the Vazonian capital."

"Do I hear a second for the General's motion?" asked the moderator.

"Second," said a number of translators.

"Then the council will now hold a vote," said the moderator. "Please vote on whether or not to grant the General permission to head for the Vazonian capital."

The General waited as the council voted. After a few moments, the moderator brought the gavel down on his podium.

"By a unanimous vote, the motion passes," said the moderator. "We will take the war to the capital."

II: "The revolution has begun," said Grand General Sazún. "The people of the empire have finally awakened."

"What will be our next move, sir?" asked General Hatshenya.

"We will ensure that the Queen's military remains focused on maintaining order," said Sazún. "If the empire remains focused on the people, then it will allow the Union to overwhelm them. You know what happened on Issius, General: before we even arrived, the people had taken to the streets. They had decided to take their lives into their own hands and they had chosen fight for their right to make their own decisions. And when we did arrive, there was nothing the Vazonian guard could do. They were no match for the combined strength of the Union, the resistance, and the people. I believe that Issius was the beginning of a chain reaction, General. I believe that it's now only a matter of time for the empire to fall."

"What does General Ulysses say?" asked General Hatshenya.

"He has gone before the Interstellar Council to ask for permission to attack the heart of the Vazonian Empire," said Sazún. "Once we acquire a nearby base of operations, of course."

Alexander Rebelle

III: Jason exhaled and looked down into Danya's eyes as they explored the boundaries of their inherent longing together in a unison of relieving intensity. She smiled lovingly at him as he groaned and reached the resounding harmony of his urging fulfilled, cast messily adrift across the hanging dunes of her sculpted posture where she knelt to be poised to the fullest delight of the soothing warmth. It raged on as rising tide of absolution for a moment, but then it faded away slowly as if freed to live on with the mountain wind around them. Jason gently eased Danya to her feet and kissed her tenderly before sitting down on the dirt with his back to a boulder. Danya did the same beside him.

"Even Sabenya couldn't make me feel like that," said Jason. "Maybe it's just because I love you, but I've never felt like that."

Jason pulled his pants back up over his hips. Neither he nor she had removed any of their clothing. Her top hung open and her skirt had migrated upward to cover only her midsection during the course of their evening exploration. Danya paused for a moment, but then pulled her skirt back into its proper place just over her hips, leaving her top open for a moment more as she smiled at Jason, then drawing across the uplifting warmth of the gentle delight still scattered recklessly about the casual drifts held comfortably up high within the grasp of her reach in light of the rising full moon. She then tied her top closed and held his hand in hers. He shook his head.

"You're amazing," he said. "For an American man, it's beautiful to see."

Jason kissed Danya.

"Such a beautiful moon," said Danya. "Vazakanya doesn't have a moon. There's another planet closer to our central star that has a moon. But it's not even close to the size of this one."

"I guess on Earth, we take it for granted," said Jason. "It's always up there: same face, same phases: it's very predictable. But every now and then, there is an eclipse. And when that happens, people do take notice."

"That must be beautiful," said Danya.

"Maybe you can see one sometime," said Jason. "Maybe after the war is over. Have you heard what's happening out there? Your mother is using her military just to keep her people from rising up against her."

"I'm actually worried," said Danya. "That they'll get to her before I do."

"You're afraid they'll storm the palace and try to do what they did to the governor of Issius?" asked Jason.

"Yes," said Danya. "I need to confront her soon. But I know Zerpanya will never let me get too close."

"Then you'll have to take on Zerpanya," said Jason. "I'm sure you could find the strength to take her down."

"Her fighting skills are superior to mine," said Danya. "No matter how you look at it. She gives my mother her power. Without Zerpanya, my mother never could have become Queen of the empire."

"Be strong," said Jason. "I believe in you. Do you believe in yourself?"

"This is the Director herself we're talking about," said Danya. "Director Zerpanya: a great innovator to the art of of Kano-Vunto. It's an ancient martial art, but she perfected it. No one can take her on and live."

"I once took her eye," said a voice. Jason and Danya turned to look back. Ex-General Kufán stood at the entrance of the base.

"You're the reason she has an electronic eye?" asked Danya. "How did you do it?"

"I tried to kill her," said Kufán. "She and I were in love. We were the highest-ranking officials in the entire empire. But our lust for power drove us apart. Ultimately, she was slightly the better fighter, but I lived to say I'd taken her eye."

"How did you live after that?" asked Danya.

"It was nothing more than a domestic dispute," said Kufán. "The Queen wanted to put me to death. Zerpanya, however, decided that she'd rather see me live the rest of my days in shame. Perhaps she still had compassion for me."

"You're trained in the ways of Kano-Vunto?" asked Danya.

"Zerpanya and I would spar with each other every day," said Kufán. "She was always better than I was, but she shared all of the insight about the martial art that she had."

"If one were ever to beat her," said Danya. "How could it be done?"

"It could be done," said Kufán. "But the answer to your question requires that I show you."

"I need to know," said Danya. "If I'm to get to my mother, I'll have to go through Zerpanya."

"Then come with me," said Kufán. "I can't make you a better fighter, but I can teach you her tendencies and attack patterns."

IV:

The sound of gunfire echoed across the streets. In the city square, a man lay dead among the protestors, having been fired upon by the Vazonian guard.

[Who's next?] yelled the guard. [Who else will defy the orders of the Queen?]

[I will,] yelled a woman. She stepped forward. [Kill me,] she yelled. [Show me your faith in Xiaf. Or are you forbidden from murdering a woman?]

The guard said nothing. The woman stepped forward. [Issius fell in less than a day,] she said. [If I were you, I'd run, run as far away as you can.]

The woman punched the guard, breaking his nose. He dropped his weapon and the woman picked it up.

[We will take no more of this,] she yelled. [Remember Issius.]

The crowd cheered. The Vazonian guards threw tear gas. A man picked the canister up and threw it back at the guards.

[Kill them all,] yelled the woman.

The people ran at the guards. The guards held their ground, but then looked at each other and began running away. The crowd began chanting

"Kolanto su no podavento, kolanto su no podavento, kolanto su no podavento," they said.

V: Grand General Sazún turned his head as a young officer rushed into the command center.

"Sir," he said. "The people of Taskurtar have revolted."

"Taskurtar," said Sazún. "That system is in the Taskurtán Sector. It's right next door to the former Vazakanian Empire."

"We must alert General Ulysses immediately," said Hatshenya.

VI: General Ulysses walked into the Pentagon. Harmony stood there.

"Sir," she said. "An urgent message from Grand General Sazún. He would like to speak with you immediately."

"Is this good or bad?" asked General Ulysses.

"It sounded good," said Harmony. "But I can't say for sure."

Ulysses hurried to the communication center.

"Put me through to the resistance," he said.

He waited as the operator contacted the base.

"General Ulysses," said Grand General Sazún. "I've found our launching point. The people of Taskurtar have revolted."

"Where is Taskurtar?" asked General Ulysses. "How close is it?"

"In the Taskurtan sector, General," said Sazún. "I'd advise that you send support in immediately. This is our chance. The resistance is already doing everything it can there."

Ulysses looked at the communication operator. "Contact the fleet," he said. "Send the fleet to Taskurtar."

VII: In the capital city, the people and the Vazonian reinforcements were at a standoff. There were hundreds of thousands of civilians in the streets. The Vazonian soldiers had set up a perimeter around the gates of the capital building. The people were throwing

stones, pipe bombs, Molotov cocktails, and many people were armed with rifles and shotguns. The people were chanting.

"Kolanto su no podavento, kolanto su no podavento, kolanto su no podavento," they chanted.

The people looked up. From the sky, a number of Vazonian assault ships drew closer and closer to the ground. The assault ships opened fire on the people. The people scattered and ran for cover.

VIII: "Alpha leader here," said the American pilot. "We're going in hard. We need to get down to that planet ASAP."

The Union fleet charged toward the Vazonian defense fleet. They began firing on each other. The carriers launched their fighters and bombers and the cruisers began firing their rail guns.

"Alpha Command to Support Squad One," said the Commander. "Head down to that planet and help those people take their planet back."

The armed personnel transports began to head for the planet with an escort of Assault ships and fighters. On board the transport at the head of the formation, a young soldier addressed the others.

"This is it, men," he said. "Are we ready to fight?"

"Let's do this," yelled one of the other soldiers.

"We're going to fight for freedom," said the first soldier. "And we will not look back."

The personnel transports entered the planet's atmosphere. Flames engulfed each one. They drew nearer and nearer to their assigned regions and they began to slow down. They landed and all of the soldiers filed out.

IX: In the capital city, the Union assault ships began to fire on the Vazonian assault ships. The people on the ground looked up: both the civilians and the Vazonian soldiers at the gates of the capital building looked up at the assault ships.

One of the Vazonian assault ships exploded. The civilians in the streets cheered. Union soldiers began to file into the central square, opening fire on the Vazonian soldiers.

X: On the streets of the planet Vazakanya, the scene was much different from what it was on the streets of every other planet in the empire. There were military checkpoints at nearly every street corner, there were more armed patrol vehicles than civilian vehicles, and very few people walked the streets.

In the basements and back rooms across the planet, however, all was not what it seemed on the surface. There were both men and women dressed in traditional Vazakanian clothing again, talking, laughing, drinking alcohol, and sitting among stockpiles of illegal weapons and armor. Down in the basement of a music supply store, a man and a woman dressed in traditional Vazakanian clothing sat at a crudely constructed wooden table surrounded by crates and boxes and a number of musical instruments.

[It's going to happen,] said the woman at the table. She sipped her beverage. [The Union is on its way.]

[I long for the days when we'll be free again,] said the man. [It is so close that I find it difficult not to think about what I will do with my freedom.]

[We must remain focused,] said the woman. [Our time will come.]

The door to the basement opened and a second woman walked down the stairs dressed in a Vazonian blue robe.

[Taskurtar has fallen to the Union,] she said. [Spread the word. The liberation is coming.]

[How do you know this?] asked the man at the table.

[No Kasanosi,] said the woman. [No Kasanosi is counting on you to supply this block of the city with weapons and armor at a moment's notice.]

[What is your name?] asked the woman at the table.

[Komanya,] said the robed woman. [What are your names?]

[I'm Normén,] said the man. [And her name is Masanya,]

[Pleasure to meet you,] said Komanya. [I must ask you: will you be ready to provide this block of the city with weapons and armor when the time to fight comes?]

[These boxes are not full of musical instruments,] said Masanya. [Every box you see contains stolen Vazonian weapons and armor.]

[You are to paint the armor green,] said Komanya. [So that the Interstellar Union can distinguish us from the Vazonian guard.]

[We will begin immediately,] said Normén. [Thank you for warning us.]

Komanya walked back up the stairs.

[We will fight for the Vazakanian Way,] said the man. [And if we are to die, then we are to die for what we believe in.]

XI: "She can never help herself," said Kufán. "She will always lead with her right. That's how I took her eye. I knew she would lead with her right. Remember that."

"I will," said Danya. "I'll look for it."

"You can tell when she turns her right side to you and slowly blinks her eyes," said Kufán. "She's about to make a move."

"What does it look like?" asked Danya. "When she does it."

Kufán crouched himself into a fighter stance. He imitated the move he'd described. Danya blocked it.

"It's a habit of hers," said Kufán. "And I never told her it was."

"Let's hope she never figured it out," said Danya.

Part III:

1:

I: The Vazonian flag was lowered from the pole. The people ripped it off the line and began stomping on it. In its place, they raised an old Taskurtán flag.

The Union soldiers saluted the people, and the people saluted back, then looking upward to the sky where in space, the Union had begun to amass a fleet of hundreds of warships, warships of all shapes and sizes. On the command deck of one, stood General Ulysses. He held the communicator to his mouth.

"People of the galaxy," he said. "The day has come. Today marks the end of the Vazonian Empire and the beginning of freedom for all who call this galaxy their home. My friends, this battle will not be easy. Do not believe for a moment that it will be. It will be a challenge like no challenge we have ever faced in our lives." He paused. "But my friends, I tell you now: this is our time. This is our moment of triumph. The time has come for us to show the Vazonian Queen the mistake she has made in trying to take our freedom from us. We will tell her that no matter what may happen in this battle, she may have taken our homes, and she may have taken our friends, and our families, and, in many cases, our pride, but I ask all of you now to remember that there is something she can never take from us. And that, my friends, is our will to fight. For the good of all humanity, I ask you humbly: fight bravely, fight boldly, and remember: this is what you live for: you live for the freedom to live your own lives. Brothers and sisters, set your course for Vazakanya. Engage on my command. You will fight for freedom."

Ulysses paused for a moment.

"Engage," said Ulysses. "To Vazakanya."

II:

Danya quietly navigated her spacecraft down to Vazakanya City. The communicator chimed.

[Incoming craft, identify yourself,] said the communicator.

[Princess Na Danya Vih Zalenya,] said Danya. [I'm here to meet the Queen.]

[Yes, she's been expecting you,] said the communicator. [You may land on the royal landing pad.]

[Thank you,] said Danya. Danya piloted the craft down onto the palace's landing pad. She exited the vessel and walked into the palace. There were no guards to be seen anywhere.

Danya made her way to the doors of the royal chamber. She opened them. The Queen sat inside on the throne with Director Zerpanya to her right.

"Hello Danya," said Zerpanya. "You've returned."

"Yes," said Danya. "I have." She looked at the Queen closely. "Who are you? You're not my mother."

"I have simply become immortal, darling," said the Queen. "This is my new body that will take the empire to eternity."

"Listen to you, mother," said Danya. "Even as your empire crumbles around you, you remain oblivious to the reality that is. It's over, mother: the Vazonian Empire has fallen. As your daughter who loves you no matter how misguided you may have become, I've come here with an offer: I wish to help you."

"Help me, Danya?" asked the Queen. "In what way? I do not need your help. My life is now eternal. I have no need for an heiress."

"An heiress of what?" asked Danya. "At this very moment, the Union and the resistance are breaking through the planetary blockade to liberate this planet. I'm offering you help, mother. As your daughter, I want to help you."

The palace shook as an explosion erupted nearby. Gunfire could be heard in the distance.

"They're coming for you, mother," said Danya. "They won't want to help you the way I want to. They'll want to destroy you."

The Queen was silent. Another nearby explosion rocked the palace. It was much closer this time.

"Mother, trust me," said Danya. "I want to help you. Come with me. I can get you the help you need."

"So naïve, Danya," said the Queen. "You will learn someday the error of your ways: your lifestyle, your beloved philosophy: it is all filth: it is a waste of a human mind. Xiaf offers you the path to eternity. Won't you join your people in following that path?"

"I pity you, mother," said Danya. "Because you now believe your own lies." Danya shook her head. "Mother, they're coming for you. They will kill you. They will take you from me. I love you too much to let that happen to you. I don't want them to take you from me." Danya paused. "As misguided as you are, mother, you raised me as your daughter, and the bond between us is the only thing that will be eternal: it is not your empire, it is not your faith, and it is not your power. It is our love."

The Queen rose from the throne. She stepped forward. Tears came to Danya's eyes. "I love you, mother," said Danya. "And I always will. Come with me. I'll help you."

"Why do you cry, Danya?" asked the Queen. "Never once in my life have I seen a tear in your eyes."

A series of explosions rocked the palace.

"Mother," said Danya. She shook her head. "They march on the palace as we speak. Don't you hear them? This is the end, mother. All that you have done in this galaxy has come to an end. There is not a single mind but my own that would wish anything but death upon you. Give me, your daughter, the only person alive who wishes to help you at the end of the Vazonian Empire, the chance to become a family with you again." The tears streamed down from Danya's cheeks. "I have found love of my own, mother. His name is Jason." Danya paused. "I would like you to meet him someday." Won't you come with me? Won't you allow us to be a family?"

The Queen was silent. She stepped forward. Zerpanya stood in her way.

"I cannot allow you to leave, your highness," said Zerpanya, "No one will leave this palace alive."

Zerpanya drew her sidearm and shot the Queen. The Queen cried out and fell to the floor. Zerpanya then began walking toward Danya with the weapon. Danya drew her own pistol. Zerpanya shot Danya's pistol out of her hand.

Danya backed toward the wall with her hands up. She looked to the altar next to her, seeing a sacrificial sword. Danya took the sword in her hands and slashed the pistol Zerpanya held. The wepon flew across the room.

"You still remember how to use it," said Zerpanya. "Well done. Drop it. Is this how you'd like it to end? You'd like to commit another sacrifice?"

Danya said nothing. She dropped the sword. "Come and get me," said Danya.

The two women began fighting. Danya was overmatched. Zerpanya threw her to the ground again and again, and Danya barely escaped each time.

Danya jumped up and watched Zerpanya lead with her right side. Danya avoided the attack. Zerpanya led with her right side again. Again, Danya avoided the attack.

Zerpanya led with her left side and Danya wasn't ready for it. She fell back against the wall. Zerpanya picked up the sacrificial sword.

Danya closed her eyes. She thought of the time she had spent with her mother as a child. She thought of Jason: all the time that they had spent together. Danya opened her eyes and covered her mouth with her left hand, pointing emphatically over the left shoulder of Zerpanya.

"What's that?" asked Danya.

Zerpanya looked behind her and Danya jumped at her, pushing her face down on the floor. Danya lifted her right foot and brought it down on Zerpanya's neck, crushing her windpipe and killing her.

Danya raced over to her mother. She was badly wounded. Danya fell to her knees and began cyring as the sound of gunfire echoed through the halls of the palace.

The doors to the chamber opened. Danya picked up her pistol and pointed it toward the entrance.

"I'll kill all of you if you try to take her from me," said Danya.

She fell silent. It was not an angry mob, but rather, a man in a mask.

"Who are you?" asked Danya. "Answer wrong, and I'll kill you."

"My name is Faustemi," said the man. "I am a healer. What has happened to the Queen?"

"She's been shot," said Danya. "Come here."

Faustemi walked over to the Queen. Her throat was severed. She could not speak. Another explosion rocked the palace violently. An loud alarm began to sound through the palace.

"Her lungs are filling with blood," said Faustemi. "She'll drown unless we can get her medical attention."

"How did she get this body?" asked Danya. "This is not my mother's body."

"Your mother?" asked Faustemi. "She's your mother?"

"Save her," yelled Danya. "Do something before the revolution comes."

Faustemi was silent for a moment. "There may be a way," he said. "We still have her original body. If we can transfer her mind back to her old body in time, then we can save her immediately. We must go to the laboratory."

Another explosion rocked the palace. The altar of Xiaf collapsed to the floor. "Quickly," yelled Danya. "Help me carry her."

Fuastemi and Danya hoisted the Queen up into their arms and began running through the palace with her.

There were more explosions. The palace shook violently once more.

"We don't have enough time," said Faustemi.

"I know a shortcut," said Danya. "Down this hallway."

They went down a hallway. They stopped at a door with a keypad. Danya punched in a sixteen-digit code. The door opened. They came to a second door. Danya closed her eyes and punched in a second code. They came to a third door. Danya remembered back to the last time she had seen the door. It had been just before she'd run away.

She closed her eyes and input the code. The door opened.

"This way," yelled Danya. She led Faustemi to the laboratory. A massive explosion shook the palace. Danya tripped and fell over. The lights dimmed. "Before it's too late," she yelled.

Fauistemi placed the dying Queen in the transfer chamber. He hurried over to the control panel and brought the machine to life. He input a series of commands to the computer and the lights dimmed. Another explosion rocked the palace, followed by another, and then another.

"It's working," yelled Faustemi. "It needs to hold together."

Danya could hear people storming the palace over the sirens, chanting, "kolanto su no podavento."

"How much longer?" yelled Danya. "They're in the palace now."

"Just another moment," yelled Faustemi.

Danya pressed her hands against the glass chamber that held her mother. She closed her eyes.

The young girl sat with Queen playing a card game.

"Remember, Danya," said the Queen. "I will always love you. No matter what may happen in the future, I am your mother and I will always love you. You may not understand what I say now, but someday you will. You're the world to me, Danya: more than all the galaxy. Someday you will understand."

Danya opened her eyes. Tears streamed down her cheeks.

"Process complete," yelled Faustemi. "She lives."

The Queen looked down at Danya from within the glass chamber. Danya picked up a chair and shattered the glass with it. She ripped her mother's life support out and took the Queen in her arms.

"To the shuttle," yelled Danya.

She and Faustemi began running toward the landing pad.

[There she is,] yelled the rebels. [Burn her.]

Danya began running faster. They came to the landing pad. She hurried up into the shuttle and lay the Queen to rest on a mattress. Faustemi made his way up the ramp just as it closed and locked, and Danya lifted the shuttle off the ground. She held the communicator to her mouth.

"Alpha fleet, this is Shadow One," said Danya. "I am now the acting Queen of the Vazonian Empire. I decree that the Vazonian Empire is dissolved, and all systems under Vazonian rule are free. Alpha Fleet, I kindly ask that you do not fire on me as I return to the Shadow Base."

"Shadow One, please give your clearance code," said the communicator.

"The remaining one," said Danya. "I am the remaining one."

"Shadow One, we copy," said the communicator. "All units, defend the Vazonian shuttle from enemy fire."

Danya watched on the monitors as a number of Union assault ships formed an escort perimeter around the shuttle. Danya looked back to Faustemi.

"How is she?" asked Danya. "Is she breathing?"

"She cannot speak," said Faustemi. "Her voice is weak. It will return in time. I cannot say how long it will take."

Danya piloted the shuttle up through the atmosphere and into space. She set a course for Earth. She engaged the time dilation drive and walked up to her mother, kneeling by her side.

"I remember what you told me, mother," said Danya. "You told me someday I would understand why you said you would always love me. I want you to know that I'll always love you too, no matter what may happen to you."

III: "Sir," said a lieutenant. "Commander Danya has returned. She calls herself the acting Queen of the Vazonian Empire. She wishes to meet you in the hangar."

"Thank you, lieutenant," said Grand General Sazún. He stepped down from the command deck and walked swiftly toward the hangar. He walked into it and looked out the entrance. In the ravine, he could see a Vazonian shuttle. It eased its way into the hangar and touched down inside. The ramp lowered. Danya walked down into the hangar.

"All hail Na Danya Vih Zalenya," said Sazún. "Queen of the Vazakanian Empire."

Danya turned and looked back as a masked man pushed a stretcher down the ramp and into the hangar.

The all-too-familiar form of Queen Jonarka lay on it. She raised her head to look at the General.

"Grand General," said Danya. "I know you've met my mother before. I offered to help her and she accepted my offer."

"The horror this woman is guilty of," said Sazún. "And you have brought her here to the base to help her."

"Vazakanians do not believe in capital punishment," said Danya. "You know that, General. We all know that. It upsets the balance of the mind. My mother needs balance. You can lock her up forever, you can throw away the key, but as long as she can be my mother, I will understand."

Grand General Sazún nodded. "She will first stand trial," he said. "As Queen of the Empire, what law do we try her under?"

"Vazakanian law," said Danya. "And she will plead guilty to everything. She will accept her sentence and she will be at peace with it."

"It would be wise to publicly address the people of the galaxy," said Sazún. "As acting Queen of the Empire. We will record you on video."

IV:

The Vazakanian flag was raised over the royal palace.

[What of the Queen?] asked Normén. [Have we found her yet?]

[We've found the corpse of Director Zerpanya,] said Masanya. [We've found the laboratory used to give her the modified body and we found what appeared to be a modified body. We don't know for sure if this body is hers or not.]

[Have we taken care to ensure that there is no looting?] asked Normén.

[The Union is doing its best,] said the Masanya. [The people of this planet have not known freedom for nearly three decades.]

[And what war it has been,] said Normén. [The lies, the hypocrisy, the mass-murder, the suffering, all because business was allowed to make its way into politics. I believe we must do everything we can to ensure that this will never happen again.]

V: "People of the galaxy, allow me to introduce myself," said Danya. "My name is Na Danya Vih Zalenya, the rightful and acting Queen of the Vazakanian Empire. I address you now to say that my predecessor has been captured and will be tried for crimes against humanity under Vazakanian Law, the law of our own people. My first act as Queen of the Vazonian Empire is to dissolve the empire. Every system my predecessor has taken by force is now free to live on its own and govern itself. I reserve my power to being Queen of the Vazakian Empire, and all ten original star systems of the Vazakanian Empire are now also free. As for the deity called Xiaf, you need not worship Xiaf unless you choose to." Danya paused. "Once my predecessor has been tried under old Vazakanian law, I will then gather the brightest minds from around the empire to assist me in rewriting the constitution so that never again can our peaceful existence be so rudely captivated by a tyrant. Once we have put in place a new government and the new government has begun to function as it should, I will declare the period of martial law to be over and I will relinquish my power to the government. I would like you to know that my predecessor now understands what she has done to the galaxy. She will plead guilty to every charge against her. I know many people around the galaxy would wish to see her be forced to give her life for her crimes, but to all the people of the empire, I ask you now: has there not been enough bloodshed? Have enough lives not been lost? To give my predecessor the penalty of death would be to make our own selves no better than she was as she committed her crimes. There is no capital punishment under Vazakanian Law, and I would humbly ask the people of the galaxy to respect the Vazakanian Way and to allow us to begin rebuilding our lives. That is my plan for the future, that is my advice to you, and I leave you now in peace. Let us all live in peace. This is Queen Na Danya Vih Zalenya wishing you good luck and a long life."

Danya rose from her seat.

"Great speech," said Jason. "You sounded a whole lot like a Queen."

2:

I: The President of the United States draped the Congressional Medal of Honor around Jason's neck. Jason saluted the President.

Danya watched the ceremony from the newly installed television set in the common room of the Shadow Base.

"Your highness," said Sabenya. "Your shuttle is in the hangar."

"Your highness," said Danya. "I'll have to get used to that. It'll take time for that to grab my attention. You don't have to call me that, Sabenya. I know you too well."

"I insist," said Sabenya. "I have a legacy to honor. Before you relinquish your power, can you give me permission to open the university again? It was the first university of the old empire and I want it to be the first university of the new empire as well."

"Go right ahead," said Danya. She rose from the couch and turned the television off, beginning to make her way to the shuttle. She and Sabenya walked into the hangar and up into the shuttle. It lifted off.

Danya looked at her mother. She sat handcuffed next to two armed guards.

"You think she'll try to escape?" asked Danya. "You had to bring this much firepower with us?"

"It's for her own safety," said Sazún. "There are many who do not want there to be a trial."

"Mother," said Danya. "Can you speak?"

Jonarka opened her mouth. She could not speak. She was unable to form words.

"Do you understand me, mother?" asked Danya.

Jonarka nodded her head.

II:

"So, Jason," said the President. "Where are you from?"

"Springfield, Massachusetts, sir," said Jason.

"Did you meet the new Queen in your time with the resistance?" asked the President.

"Actually sir," said Jason. "What I'm about to tell you, I tell you with all respect in the world, but she and I are in love and I plan on helping her rebuild the Vazakanian Empire. I'm no longer at home in this country. I'm thankful for everything it gave me in life, but it's time for me to move on. I imagine I'll come to visit often, but I belong with her now. I hope this doesn't offend you, Mr. President."

"The greatest thing about being an American," said the President, "is that you're free to make that decision, Jason. If that's what you plan to do, then I wish you luck. You will always be remembered here in this country as one of our greatest heroes."

"Thank you for understanding, Mr. President," said Jason. "I'll enjoy this fine meal your chefs prepared, and then I'll be heading off to my new home. At heart, I'll always be an American, but in spirit, I'm now Vazakanian."

III:
Danya sat in the royal box as the judge delivered the sentence.

[Na Jonarka Vih Vazonya,] said the judge. [You are hereby sentenced to live the remainder of your life in maximum security detainment. What you have done to all of humanity is unforgivable and you must pay the price for your crimes. Have you anything to say for yourself?]

Jonarka opened her mouth but, again, was unable to speak.

The judge brought the gavel down on the podium. The resistance guards cuffed Jonarka and led her out of the room. Danya rose from the royal box with Grand General Sazún, Sabenya, and General Hatshenya. They all left the courtroom.

"I think we should begin drawing up the new constitution," said Danya. "Anyone have any ideas?"

"I have many ideas," said Grand General Sazún. "I'm sure we all have many ideas. We cannot take this task lightly. We must ensure that never again can our freedom and our rights be taken from us."

IV:
General Ulysses stood before the Interstellar Council. He looked down at his notes.

"In the end," he said, "The people of the galaxy chose to take matters into their own hands. With the help of the resistance, and with our own firepower for support, the

Queen's military could not withstand the will of those she governed. From this, we can perhaps draw the conclusion that government, no matter how large or small it may be, may be defined as a measure to counteract the will of human nature. For when a single individual is allowed to control everything from the way the people live to the faith the people hold, we have seen across culture and across time that power corrupts the balance of the mind and most often brings forth the worst in human nature. In the beginning, it was industry that made its way into politics, sponsoring candidates and giving them funding for their campaigns. I ask the people of the galaxy to take note of this. I yield the floor now with these final words under my tenure as Supreme Commander of Union Forces: I would encourage the world leaders present in this assembly to let these last twenty-one years of warfare be a lesson in government and power. The choice you can make in the rebuilding of your homes is simple: you have fought bravely for liberation and freedom. And now you must decide how you will govern your freedom. There is a point at which government becomes tyranny. If you will take my words to mind, then I am confident you will make a wise decision. I yield the floor. Thank you very much."

General Ulysses stepped away from the podium.

V: Jason pushed the left side of the cart while Danya pushed the right side. The contents of the cart were golden and jewel-encrusted statues of Xiaf. They came to the door and dumped it into the dumpster.

"So this all gets melted down and goes to the treasury, which will do what for the new empire?" asked Jason.

"Gold is a precious metal everywhere," said Danya. "Sabenya has discussed this with me. While our currency is worthless at the moment, the fact that we have so much gold in the treasury should attract at least some foreign investors to fund the rebuilding of our civilization. It's not going to be easy in the beginning."

"I don't think anyone believes it will be easy," said Jason. He began pushing the cart back through the palace as Danya walked beside him. "How's the new constitution coming?"

"Very carefully," said Danya. "We're trying to learn from the mistakes of the old constitution: mostly that we allowed massive businesses to buy legislation from politicians. That won't happen again."

They came to a door with a chain and a lock on it. Danya picked up the cutter and crushed through the chain. She pulled it back and opened the door. She flipped the light on. It was a room full of shelves and shelves of ancient scrolls.

"What is it?" asked Jason.

"I think we've just discovered the original manuscript of Queen Vazakanya's Constitution," said Danya. "My mother must have locked it up."

"Why didn't she destroy it?" asked Jason.

"Maybe even she couldn't destroy something hand-written by the Great Queen Vazakanya herself," said Danya. "That's all I can guess."

3:

I: Grand General Sazún stood inside the hangar of the space station as he looked over the captured weapon.

"What is it?" he asked. "Exactly."

"It could have been the death of the resistance and the Union together, sir," said the scientist. "This is a weapon of mass destruction on a scale we have never seen before. Had it worked in the battle, it would have destroyed everything. We were very lucky that we managed to capture the plans for this weapon from the royal palace."

"We must ensure that this technology is never seen or heard of again," said Sazún. "We must destroy the plans and we must destroy the weapon."

"My only fear is that copies of the plans may be scattered across the galaxy in secret laboratories and space stations we have yet to discover," said the scientist. "They called this weapon the Tempest. It could destroy an entire world."

"Dismantle the weapon and destroy the pieces," said Sazún. "I never want to see it or hear of it again. A weapon like this is symbolic of what war does to humanity:

it brings out the best and the worst of human nature together. What an innovation a weapon like this is, and yet, how disturbing the very idea of its existence is. We must make sure that in The Legend of Humanity: The Remaining One, this weapon never becomes a chapter of our story."

"Wise words, sir," said the scientist.

"Now that the war is over," said Sazún. "We must focus on a new beginning, a fresh start for all the galaxy. It is my sincerest hope that never will there come a time when we see the face of a world destroyed."

II: Danya opened the doors to the building.

"It's a library," said Jason.

"The forbidden library," said Danya. "Where all literature about Vazakanian philosophy, science, and history is located. Every text in this building was determined to be sacrilegious."

They stepped inside and turned the main power supply on. It was a vast expanse of shelves and shelves of books.

"Your mother didn't destroy any of this either?" asked Jason.

"No," said Danya. "And I don't know why for these texts. But I'm sure there was a reason."

Danya walked up to the first aisle of books and removed one of them, opening it to the first page. Jason looked over her shoulder.

"The Vazakanian Way," said Danya. "Queen Vazakanya. This is the foundation of our civilization."

Danya put the book back. She and Jason began wandering through the building. They came to a large golden throne in the middle of the library that was locked behind a steel cage.

"Queen Vazakanya's original throne," said Danya. "This building is the original location of the first royal palace. No king or queen that followed her ever had the courage to move her throne."

Jason took the wire cutters out of Danya's hand and crushed through each of the three locks on the door. He pushed the door open and stepped forward, pulling back the rope and walking before the throne. He brushed the dust off.

"This gold looks cracked," he said.

"What do you mean?" asked Danya. She walked up to the throne. Jason pointed down at the seam on the right armrest. Danya ran her fingers along the seam. She pulled at it. The portion of the armrest swiveled up, revealing a small compartment. There was a small but very thick book inside. Danya removed the book and looked down at the first page. She read it out loud.

"To whomever it may interest, this album contains a collection of images from the life of her Highness, Queen Vazakanya, taken and compiled by her loving daughter, Zalenya," said Danya. "It is the sincere hope of Queen Vazakanya that whomever may discover this album will kindly respect it as her legacy."

Danya flipped the page. It was a grainy color image of Queen Vazakanya as she addressed an assembly of people. Danya and Jason stared at the photo. They stared at it for a long moment.

"The people," said Jason. "Look at them."

"They look like," said Danya. She paused.

They stared at the picture for a short moment more.

"They look like my own people," said Jason. "Diverse, different from one another in many ways, and free to be as they are. They look just like the people of Earth."

Author's Note Post Script

I sincerely thank you for reading this text. It is my firm belief that, in time, people will understand what it stands for. This is the second work of fiction I have released as an author, but it is, in reality, the first work I began seriously writing. I began working on *The Harmony Passion* once I had completed Part I of this book and had become frustrated with my inability to create Part II to the point at which I simply needed a break from this book altogether. And now that you've read this book, I will momentarily go about providing you with some free omniscient background information. If you're very familiar with, and well-versed in books and literature, then the information I'm about to discuss will not be anything you don't already know. You'll have figured it out because you'll know how to read between the lines and think about what you're reading. But just so I don't have the layman ceaselessly begging me to give my characters telekinetic powers in any of my future work, then here are the answers to your questions written in detail below.

In the year 2045, scientists on Earth discovered the technology that would allow humans to easily travel through the interstellar medium in a very timely fashion.

It turns out the secret was all in thermonuclear fusion with the added factor of rotation. You see, if an object in space is traveling fast enough with enough rotation, then the rotation will drag a bubble of general relativistic reality with the spacecraft as it travels. The first unmanned mission to Alpha Centauri shocked the people on Earth with the presence of an unidentified object orbiting around the star that seemed perfectly cylindrical. Many scientists sought to dismiss the object as a product of an out-of-focus lens on the camera. Some scientists, however, jumped to the conclusion of intelligent life present within the system. The object was never seen again by the probe, however, so over time, the controversy died down.

Two years later in 2047, though, scientists sent another probe to the star system. And the images it returned were at first thought to be a hoax but were later proven when the fleet of spacecraft captured on them showed up in orbit around Earth. So, when this happened, people were a' freakin' out. The moon was full at the time (symbolism) and the fleet of spacecraft had deliberately placed themselves to eclipse the moon (further symbolism). Across the globe, the radio staion 99.9 FM on the night of the full moon began broadcasting a message spoken perfectly in the dialect of each radio station's region, and the messenger claimed to be the voice of an organization called the Interstellar Union. The message was long and probably could have been shorter, but in essence, it laid out the reality of the universe. The reality of the universe is that only an absolute, narrow-minded, brainwashed, and brain-dead idiot would ever believe that intelligent life occurred in only a single place in the entire universe. Patterns in the natural universe repeat themselves very often. How many things do you know of in the universe that there is only one of? I'm talking to the scientists out there. Seriously, scientists: you can think of no other phenomenon that only exists in one case throughout the entire universe, and yet it's preposterous to you to say that humans can't possibly be alone. Please. Open your eyes already. Open your eyes. Anyway, I'm done talking to the scientists now. They can go back to creating useless forms of artificial matter in their particle accelerators or whatever it is they were doing at the time.

So, as I was saying, once the scientists on the planet Earth felt like complete idiots because that's exactly what a lot of them were, regardless of their PHDs and high IQs, the people of Earth learned that their planet was a very popular oxygen recharge station for the rest of the galaxy. So, basically, all of the ancient alien theories were proven correct. UFOs did exist. And all around the world, ancient aliens had taken advantage of the poor and more-primitive ancient people of Earth by convincing the people of Earth to worship them as Gods. So, again, scientists and intellectuals felt like total idiots. Not everything could be explained, however. When the leaders of Earth met the Interstellar Union ambassadors, the leaders of Earth were shocked to find that all of the intelligent life around our particular galaxy was, well, human. Yeah, they weren't quite aliens in the way people on Earth had traditionally imagined them. They were pretty much other human beings that looked like us, walked like us, talked like us, and were even capable of reproducing with us. So that was a mystery no one really understood, and as of the end of this book, no one really does understand it. Some theorized that the human form was somehow the highest possible form of intelligent life that could exist in nature, but the same ancient alien theorists that had correctly thought there was something odd about all the pyramid-shaped monoliths and the massive dolomite ruins at Tiwanaku that could have only been cut with dimond-tipped stone cutting tools, once again began a' cookin' up some more crackpot theories. Everyone loves crackpot theories. Here are a few of them: this galaxy was originally used a sort of slave farm for an even higher form of intelligent life possibly from another galaxy. How 'bout that one, huh? Well, here's another one: it's the same concept: higher form of intelligent life from somewhere else, but humans weren't supposed to be slaves; they were a scientific experiment intended to be used as research on the progression and advancement of intelligent life and civilization. That's a good one, isn't it? Here's one more to chew on: God did it. Yeah, it was all the work of some sort of deity. And now that you've heard this third theory, I'm sure you understand why I've portrayed the galaxy the way I have in my work.

So, as I said, for the people of the Milky Way Galaxy, there is no clear reason why all intelligent life there is human. Queen Jonarka certainly convinces her people, and eventually herself, to believe in one of those three theories, which you obviously know from reading this story, right? You did actually read it, didn't you? You didn't just read this author's note postscript because you heard it was crazy, did you? I won't deny being crazy. That's what I am and I'm proud of it: I'm crazy. I'm like a turkey stuffed with duck and chicken: it's all crazy. And I'm dangerous too because I'm pretty damn smart for a crazy person.

If any of my work ever becomes popular, I know exactly how people will react to it. First of all, those citizens of the United States that tend to have a certain mentality that I'm sure anyone politically aware would know, would absolutely despise me, my work, and anything that has to do with me. Now, these people I speak of would most likely classify this particular book as something along the lines of a "leftist, Marxist, socialist, or facist manifesto meant to destroy the fabric of the greatest country God gave man." I'm rather certain these people would use at least a few of those words to describe this book. These people tend throw the words 'socialist' and 'facist' at any popular political or cultural movement they don't like, and the thing about them that I find hilarious is that these people tend to have no understanding of these two words in practice. These people seem to feel that any progressive sort of thinking is somehow going to lead the United States of America toward becoming something in the image of the Vazonian Empire I've depicted in this book. They seem to buy into the concept of moral absolutism: the belief that there is a universal standard by which right and wrong can be judged across time and culture. Curiously, though, the universal standard tends to be their own personal beliefs at the time. I won't name names, but if my work ever becomes popular, then I know exactly who is going to voice the opinion that I'm a radical, leftist, Marxist, communist, facist, socialist, and anarchist all at the same time somehow.

I'll tell you what I really believe right here to avoid all the controversy. I would like to voice my beliefs right here and right now. I would like to make a modest proposal (symbolism) that would fix the current political system in America. I propose that we create a constitutional amendment that would allow only women with at least five years of experience in the adult entertainment industry to hold political office. You see, female adult entertainers know the darkest and most primitive side of humanity.

I reason that this job requirement will absolutely limit the number of fraudulent people that could make their way into public office. Yes, that is my modest proposal (symbolism), and I believe it will work very fully. Of course, if this solution seems slightly too radical to the good people of America, then I would offer you my 'Plan B.' My backup plan is not nearly as good or as sexy of an idea as my first idea, but I figure it could work out. And the basic concept of this plan would be to outlaw the practice of partisan politics and political campaign donations by corporations, whteher indirectly through special intrest groups and lobbies, or directly now that it's legal. Political parties would become illegal and would be considered acts of political collusion. That's a given. For two or more political figures to make an agreement to somehow unite and gain an advantage over all other politicians would be considered corruption. And, of course, there could only be publicly funded political campaigns. Real people would fund the campaigns of candidates. There would be no corporations, no special interest groups, and no lobbyists in the equation. Of course, this idea doesn't have nearly the sex appeal of the first idea, and I'd even be so bold as to say this plan B is far less likely to happen than plan A as well, but I figured I'd need a backup plan if no one liked my first idea. This plan B would have to come in the form of constitutional amendments though. Politicians couldn't be trusted not to repeal either law if it were just legislation.

But then again, a larger problem is simply the culture in the United States of America: the feeling of superiority, the sense of entitlement: just because I paid for something, I deserve it more than you do. Did you know that if Americans didn't ever pay any taxes, oh, say,

North Korea could invade and conquer us in a matter of days? We'd have no military, no governing body, and no one to calm everyone down in a time of crisis. Although, no government would also allow a completely unregulated free market. So if that would happen, then perhaps North Korea wouldn't be able to invade, because we'd have an anarchical society full of defense contractors like Vazonya Incorporated. You did get that right? Queen Jokarka began as an executive for a defense contractor: arming and sponsoring your lives since 5487. Vazonya: your friendly neighborhood human life sponsor / defense contractor. Together, we can destroy our enemies and achieve eternity through corporate donations to the political campaigns of politicians. So go ahead: eliminate taxes altogether. Be my guest. It would be an honor to die at the hands of an unregulated free market. It would validate what I've tried to do in my work.

But where was I in the background story? Oh yeah. So, long story short, the U.N. Security council voted to join the Interstellar Union later in 2047, which had the fringe benefits of increased taxes and a Union-funded interstellar transit authority that would take anyone on Earth to any other planet in the Union. Oh yeah, and there was all the military power of the Union too. That was a very convincing factor. Think about it: the people on Earth now realized that the entire galaxy was civilized. And the people on Earth had nothing designed to defend the planet from an interstellar invasion. The people on Earth felt defenseless and vulnerable. But, if you read the story and didn't just read this author's note post script, then you'd know it just happened to work out in Earth's favor. Oh, and in the interest of clarifying the time period for these two works, *The Harmony Passion* takes place between the years of 2082 and 2083 on the planet Earth, which is just over thrity years after Earth joined the Union. Apollo and Sonya are not old enough to remember life before Earth entered its Galactic Age. This is just to be clear.

Now, no one has ever left the Milky Way Galaxy and has returned. Some have tried to get into the Andromeda Galaxy, and in a few cases, that Sculptor Galaxy they don't teach you about in school for some reason, but no one knows what happened to any of those people. Some theorize that our galaxy may be surrounded by antimatter and have offered antimatter as the explanation as to why we'd been unable to understand the lack of antimatter in the universe, but that's all anyone can really come up with.

As I say in the Author's Note at the beginning of the book, this story takes place about fifty years after the summer of 2083 on the planet Earth, which, if you can do math, means that the year is now roughly 2133. Curiously, as Apollo and Sonya would point out, being so involved in the world of music, this means that the year in which The Vazonian Empire went to war with the Interstellar Union to start the Galactic War was the year 2112. Of course, by that time, the band was finally in the hall of fame and had finally gotten the credit it deserved. You know the band I'm talking about. No, not Snow Goose. Look it up, people.

Anyway, you may be wondering where Sonya and Apollo are in all of this story. I mean, they'd only be in their mid-seventies age-wise, and because it's the future, people will certainly live longer and healthier lives by then, right? Well, the thing about that is, well, information about my universe comes on a need to know basis. You do not yet need to know that. Perhaps you will in time. What else might people desperate for background information want to know? Thinking. Thinking.

Oh. And yeah, the Vazakanian language is very real. I have an entire dictionary and grammar rulebook I've invented. Verbs in the language conjugate, and there is only a single conjugation. Maybe I'll publish the translation key someday. Linguists I've shown it to and have spoken it to say it has no syntax. Um, it's an alien fucking language. Of course it doesn't have the syntax you're used to with languages on Earth. The background story for my universe is very thought out. It's much like a movie. And I'll tell you now: people who read *The Harmony Passion* said that it would make a perfect movie because of the way I believe in "show but don't tell." So, if this ever happens for either book, here are my contractual demands for the production company:

1: I will be co-director. I'm not going to pretend I know anything about directing a film and I'm not going to act like I do when it happens, but I'd damn well better have the power to approve or reject the way you choose to portray any of my work. My co-director will do all of the directing, but if I see any Hollywood sensationalizing of anything I've written in either book, I will not allow it to happen. You have no idea how much I despise what cinema has become in today's world.

2: The movie will only use CGI where I approve it. I'll tell you now how all of the battles in space will be created just so we're on the same page. We're going to be using plastic models. We're not going to use CGI to create the warships, the planets, or the space stations. Why? Because I want it all to look real, and, to my eyes, there is no CGI that looks 100% real. If you're a director and you're reading this, you're probably cringing right now as you read this, so I'll have you know that I will not hesitate to refuse seven or eight figure offers to make either movie if all three of my demands are not met.

3: I'd like a trailer with my name on the door and a bowl of taffy on the table, but no banana taffy. If there's ever banana taffy in the bowl, then I'll pull the plug on the project.

These are my demands for any sort of movie. I probably feel most strongly about the third demand. I can't stand banana-flavored candy: tastes nothing like banana. So what else is there to settle about my work? What else? What else?

Right. The character of Sonya Sweet in *The Harmony Passion* is based on no one in particular. There are many similarities between her and a number of popular female adult entertainers, and I've heard people, mostly men, playing a sort of guessing game with me as to who Sonya must really be in our world. She's no one in particular. But I will say that the whole idea to make a female adult entertainer into a protagonist in a story was inspired by a very good personal friend of mine. She uses the name Heather Summers in her work, and she is one of the most admirable people I have ever met in my life. She and I have corresponded with one another through email for a very long time now. I have learned much about the stigma and the stereotyping that comes with her profession, and it has always bothered me that people in mainstream society frown on people like her without even knowing her personally. Adult entertainers are people, you know. Everyone is a person. They have personalities and they eat and sleep and breathe just like you do. I think it's time we allow them the equality they're guaranteed in this country under that often-forgotten document we call the constitution. Seriously, relations between the adult entertainment community and mainstream society may as well be where they were pre-civil rights era. They have progressed nowhere since adult entertainment was allowed to exist in this country. This might have flown over your head in reading the two books I've written so far, but I believe strongly in working for equality, and not just that legal obligation kind of equality. I'm talking about the kind of equality in which parents no longer fear for the safety and or moral integrity of their children when simply in the presence of those members of society who are somehow different from a majority of others in society. That's what I'm talking about.

Anyway, that's all the omniscient information you're going to get in this book. Keep in mind that all of this only applies to the universe in my mind and the universe in my mind is not the universe we live in. So if you have a problem with anything I've said, it doesn't apply to this universe. It's fiction. The idea that anything could change for the better in the world we live in so quickly is fiction. It only applies to the universe in my mind like I said. I want to stress that. Thank you again for reading this book. If you'd like more omniscient information and background about my universe, then feel free to read the book again, but this time concentrate. Until next time, always feel free to take on life.